THE MORTIFICATION
OF FOVEA
MUNSON

Mary Winn Heider

Disney • HYPERION

LOS ANGELES   NEW YORK

First Edition, June 2018

10 9 8 7 6 5 4 3 2 1

FAC-020093-18110

Printed in the United States of America

This book is set in 13-pt Adobe Devanagari/Fontspring; Badneighborhood,
Ellipse ITC Std, Feltpen Pro, Vag Rounded LT Pro/Monotype
Designed by Maria Elias
Illustrations by Chi Birmingham

Library of Congress Cataloging-in-Publication Data
Names: Heider, Mary Winn, author.
Title: The Mortification of Fovea Munson / Mary Winn Heider.
Description: First edition. • Los Angeles ; New York : Disney-Hyperion, 2018.
Summary: Forced to help in her parents' cadaver lab for the summer,
Fovea Munson, twelve, discovers three talking heads in need of a favor.
Identifiers: LCCN 2017025226 • ISBN 9781484780541 (hardcover) •
ISBN 148478054X (hardcover)
Subjects: CYAC: Dead—Fiction. • Head—Fiction. • Supernatural—Fiction.
• Medical laboratories—Fiction. • Friendship—Fiction.
• Family life—Illinois—Chicago—Fiction. • Chicago (Ill.)—Fiction.
Classification: LCC PZ7.1.H443 Mor 2018 • DDC [Fic]—dc23
LC record available at https://lccn.loc.gov/2017025226

Reinforced binding

Visit www.DisneyBooks.com

For Karl and Malie

1.

HIPPOCRATES
NEVER HAD TO CALL
FAMILY MEETINGS

Dead bodies are the worst.

I've been trying to explain that to my parents for years. Mostly, I don't come right out and say it, but sometimes I can't help myself.

The main problem is that they just don't seem to get it.

I'll say: "Dead bodies are the worst."

They'll say: "Fovea! They're so *helpful*! There's nothing better than a good, *helpful* dead body!"

"Especially," my dad might say.

"When you need a hand!" my mom will finish. Then the two of them probably high-five over the dinner table, giggling.

On the other side of the table, Grandma Van will have fallen asleep over her turkey slab. It's a sort of protest, I think.

Then dinner just keeps going while my dad talks about a knee he was really fond of, and my mom wonders if the shoulder they have in the freezer at work will be muscly enough, and I try to figure out how I keep failing quite so badly.

And how the heck I wound up in this family.

The truth is, there's nothing wrong with my parents that a dead body can't fix. Except for their cheerfulness issues. I'm not sure anything can fix their cheerfulness issues.

And anyway, after everything that's happened, I can confirm that dead bodies are absolutely *not* helpful in any way whatsoever. Also, I think that stuff is gross, and I want to be clear about it, so you don't think I'm into gross stuff. It's exclusively my parents who are seriously into gross stuff.

They're surgeons. They used to be regular surgeons, and then they stopped all that so they could have a better schedule. The regular surgeons of the world sometimes have to race to the hospital in the middle of the night to do random surgeries. But that's only an issue if your patients are ALIVE. So these days, my mom and dad do surgeries on dead people. Completely predictable dead people.

Sorry. *Cadavers.*

My parents love the cadaver biz. They get to work normal business hours and have a regular schedule. They get to teach eager med students who are excited to practice surgeries. They deal exclusively with dead patients, who, as a bonus, will never argue with them. Also, as you may have noticed, there's the death-defying wordplay.

And that never stops.

There's also my name. In medical lingo, my first name, Fovea, means "eyeballs."

Right.

They named their only kid "Eyeballs."

And it's not like I can go by my middle name either. It's Hippocrates. Super catchy, I know. They're obsessed with the original Hippocrates, aka the Father of Modern Medicine, and even though he's been dead for over two thousand years, our apartment is a shrine to the guy. His picture is everywhere: T-shirts, soaps, even the toilet seat. I was the only kid with a Hippocrates backpack in kindergarten. They have matching tattoos with Hippocrates' favorite slogan, "Do No Harm." They can't get enough of him, and they've been trying to get me on board since the day I was born.

I'm onto them. It's all part of their plan for me to follow in their weirdo footsteps. They opened a tiny cadaver lab of their very own, buried right in the heart of Chicago, and aside from the students and the occasional experimenting surgeons who come in to do the practice surgeries with them, the lab staff is pretty small—it's really just my parents and Whitney, who's the receptionist and has been pre-premed for like six years. Or that's how it was, until Whitney got a new life goal that did not involve dead people, took off to Florida with her boyfriend one day, and left my parents up a creek.

The note she left said:

Dean and I are going to go big time. Srry for the bummer. This bird's gotta sing. Miami ho.

It was a weird little note. My dad put it on the fridge, next to the magnet of **Hippocrates' Cooking Guide to Ounces and Pounds**. "Beginnings," he said with a sigh. He gets sentimental easy.

Anyway, right about then *I* was all about *endings*. School was finally almost out, and it had been a really lousy school year, so I was pumped to be leaving seventh grade in the dust. At home, I had this massive ongoing packing situation for the sleepaway camp I was supposed to go to for most of the summer. It was going to be great. Sure, I'd probably end up with poison ivy and get lost in the woods and fall off a horse. But despite that, camp was the one thing my parents and I agreed on. They were happy about me learning camp-related skills, and I was happy that no one there wanted me to grow up and become a doctor. So, like every year, I was off to camp.

Or at least I was until a few days before school was out, when we got a letter in the mail that there had been this whole boom in the snake population, a total snake infestation, all in the camping huts, or whatever, and they were closing the camp.

"Well, this is a nightmare," my mom said.

"Yeah, too bad," I said.

"How can they do this?" she said.

"They probably just got tired of living in the woods," I said.

She sighed. "I was not referring to the snakes."

I decided it would be a good moment to go to my room and dump out my half-filled suitcase.

I was wrong. While I was unpacking, my parents had the kind of brilliant idea that makes me wish I could go live in a camping hut with a bunch of snakes.

It made perfect sense, they explained as they got dinner ready. There I was, inconveniently out of a summer plan, and there they were, inconveniently out of a receptionist now that Whitney had left, and, wait for it . . . they'd decided I was old enough to work a part-time job at the family business.

I was opposed to this idea, on account of it not being 1955.

And also, *the bodies.*

I leaned against the kitchen counter for support, knowing they expected me to be thrilled. My mom thwacked her knife into a tomato, its seedy guts spurting out across the cutting board. My dad set a timer and wiped his hands. The ominous smell of sloppy joes hung in the air.

Bodies. Guh.

My dad's apron stared back at me. Hippocrates was on it, naturally. A speech bubble over his smiling face said SURGEONS KNOW THE BEST CUT.

Even the apron was out to get me.

"Or," I offered, "I could stay at home."

"Nope." Having massacred enough tomatoes for sloppy joe toppings, my mom wiped off her hands and started digging around in the junk drawer. "We don't want you home alone all summer. And sweetheart—just imagine how much quality time we can spend together. AHA!" She pulled out a pair of nail clippers and held them up in the air like she'd just invented them. My dad clapped. They're always encouraging each other.

"I could stay at somebody *else's* house? Like with … a friend?" I didn't technically have those types of friends anymore, but I wasn't giving up so easily.

"Ooh! We can have lunch as a family every day!" said my mom. Apparently, she wasn't giving up so easily either. The situation didn't look good. It was time to get serious. Thankfully, the sloppy joes still had a few more minutes. I suggested an emergency family meeting, and the three of us moved to the dinner table. My mom brought along her clippers. My dad picked up a lint roller. I wished they could stay focused.

"Regarding my summer plans," I began as we all sat down. "Please please please don't make me work in the lab. I'll go to any kind of camp. Anything. That wilderness camp."

My mom took off her glasses and de-smudged them with the bottom of her shirt. "Sweetheart," she said, "the whole time you were at wilderness camp, you never actually stepped out into the wilderness."

"I loved that wilderness camp. It was just, you know. My allergies."

"You're allergic to latex, honey." She put her glasses back on. "There isn't much latex in the wild."

"There is latex at *the lab*, though, right?" I asked. Maybe I had an out. "Working in the lab might be hazardous to my health." I put a hand to my forehead. "Maybe it already is. I'm feeling woozy."

"Nah." My mom smiled. "You'll be fine. The only latex is way in back—"

My dad smiled, picking up the cue. "And that area's off-limits until you're in med school, like all the other—"

"Future Doctors of America!" they said in unison.

This would have been a perfect opportunity to mention that I really didn't *want* to be a Future Doctor of America. But I'd already been stalling for twelve years. Why stop now?

"Or maybe . . ." I said, trying to bring it back down, "maybe you could send me back to that pottery camp?"

They turned to look at the shelf holding approximately seventy-five handmade ceramic coasters I'd made at pottery camp. It was a pretty wobbly stack since none of the coasters were actually flat.

"I think," my dad said, turning his attention back to peeling off the top layer of sticky paper from the lint roller, "that we're probably okay on drink coasters."

I tried one more. "Theater camp?"

"You had all those nightmares about *Hamlet*." My mom shuddered. "I don't think any of us want to go through that again. That is definitely *not to be*." The two of them tried not to giggle. They failed.

I was desperate. "The cadaver lab has *cadavers*," I said. They nodded matter-of-factly.

I tried to break it down for them. "This is the kind of thing that scars people for life. Forever. I mean, *death*. I'd be in the lobby, right down the hall from it. Deathly death stuff."

"I prefer to think of the lab as a life-giving place," my mom said. "Where the phoenix rises from the ash."

"Where the earth cycle blooms brightest," said my dad. They both nodded earnestly.

I broke it down for them. "It's gross. It's really, really gross."

"It's not gross," my mom said as she started clipping her fingernails so she wouldn't get dead person tissue under them.

"It's noble," my dad said as he lint-rollered his head so that none of his hair would land inside a body he was opening up. In his spare time, my dad was balding.

"And," my mom added, "it's fun!" *Clip. Clip.*

"Can't we try some other camps? *Any* kind of camp?"

"Oh, honey!" My mom put down the clippers. "Who needs camp when you can have..." She looked toward my dad expectantly.

It only took him a second. "*Hippo*campus!" They high-fived.

"That's in the brain," my mom explained, pointing at her own brain for clarification. "Oh, Fo, this is going to be so great! And all your friends will be jealous!"

They didn't even seem to notice I was arguing with them.

Ding! went the timer.

They leapt up and swept into the kitchen to deal with dinner. As I watched them go, my dad leaned toward my mom and whispered, "Everything we've ever wanted!"

I was pretty sure he wasn't referring to the sloppy joes.

What was I going to say?

I'll tell you what I was thinking, though:

Some people's parents own ice-cream stores.

HIPPOCRATES
NEVER HAD
DIGNITY ISSUES IN
SCIENCE CLASS

So, update: all my friends were not jealous.

Actually, I did not mention my new summer plans to any of my friends at school.

Actually, I was a little short on friends.

I'll back it up.

School had officially started going down the toilet for me four months ago, when my best friend in the world cut me loose in one spectacular moment of glory. It's that classic, age-old problem where the friendship blossoms and grows and changes and then one person's not into it anymore and stops talking to you and you feel like a piece of old sandwich meat and then everybody at school is suddenly calling you Igor.

Or maybe that's just me.

"Igor!" Devon Kovach called from across the science lab.

Lucky me, the name had stuck.

"Igor!"

It had stuck all the way to the last day of school, so there I was in my final science class of seventh grade, ignoring Devon Kovach and not telling anyone at all about my new summer plans.

It wasn't like people were asking, though. The classroom was total chaos.

Ms. Peters wanted to use up all of her leftover supplies, so everybody was working on a different project. Groups of twos and threes stood around the tall lab tables, working on whatever kit they'd snagged.

I was sharing a table with the Lauras. The Lauras were inseparable—people said it all the time. Their teachers said it; other teachers said it. Mostly teachers said it, I guess. The Lauras and I were more what you'd call "separable."

They'd let me hang out with them since third grade, but then I drifted away when I met Em. The Lauras weren't adjusting well to me being back. I got it. And honestly, I was willing to overlook a lot on account of the coincidence of them both being named Laura. The Lauras even had a motto about being a Laura: "Like twins, but with more DNA."

"And fewer names!" I added once. They did not laugh. They pretty much never laughed, as far as I could tell. They'd always been mysterious, somehow without being interesting. But they were still better than being alone.

That last day of school in Ms. Peters's class, they'd picked up a kit that looked perfect for them. It was called "How to Use Your Own DNA to Code Your Way Out of a Theoretical Escape Room." I dropped my stuff at the table with them and one Laura glanced meaningfully at the other Laura.

I got it. If they wanted space, I could give them space. I guess it could've been my imagination, but it seemed like they were taking more of it than usual.

Anyway, that was how I ended up in a group of one with a kit called "How to Use Basic Physics to Send Objects Hurtling Through Space With Specificity."

"Igor! Igooor!" Devon hollered for me again. "Look!"

Ms. Peters, either oblivious or trying to be, sat behind her desk with her nose buried in one of those novels where a virus gets loose and destroys the world.

"Looook!" Devon was at the "How to Dissect Virtually Anything" table, which unfortunately sat right in my line of vision. "The monster! It's aliiiive!" He held his half-dissected frog by its skinny little arms and made the frog stagger across the tray in my direction. Kylie, his lab partner, laughed so hard she couldn't even stand up. The rest of my class thought it was pretty hilarious, too.

I was more on the frog's side of things.

Across from me, the Lauras quietly congratulated each other about getting through Round One of the theoretical escape room and mumbled something I couldn't quite make out about me and dignity.

I am WORKING on dignity, I wanted to say, *it's just a little hard these days*, but then I glanced over exactly in time to see the frog's intestines fall out, and I realized that pretty much summed up how I felt, and anyway it was the last day of school, and sometimes, when things were intestines-falling-out bad and seventh grade was almost over forever, it had to be okay to just give up. One of those moments where you focus instead on how eighth grade is going to be completely different and your intestines will be totally fine once you get there. Hopefully.

So, with eighth grade on my mind, I pretended I hadn't heard the Lauras.

Doing his best at a loud, ribbity grunt, Devon made the frog karate-kick and Kylie cheered.

"Devon, Kylie," said Ms. Peters wearily over the cover of her book. "Is there a problem?"

The main problem, in my opinion, was that I couldn't fast-forward through the rest of this day. I pulled back the small catapult I'd built and let it go. The lump of clay was supposed to fly over the table, but instead, when the belt snapped, my tablespoon of clay flopped directly onto the table with a resounding *splat.*

In my defense, I *might* have done a better job if I wasn't so distracted. And I'm not even talking about the frog situation.

Specifically: that family meeting yesterday had been a flat-out disaster. I could not spend my whole summer in the lab. I just couldn't.

I mean, sure, *probably* my parents weren't going to make me dig up graves and drag body parts home for their creepy experiments. But these were the facts: my cadaver-appreciating parents were basically nerdy, married versions of Dr. Frankenstein. And now I was going to be helping them. For four months, everybody at school had been calling me Igor, and for four months I'd been counting on a clean-slate summer, a shake-it-off summer, a start-eighth-grade-with-no-obvious-baggage summer, and no way could I shake off the rumor that I was Dr. Frankenstein's body-slinging assistant Igor if I WAS ACTIVELY BEING AN IGOR.

Plus, I'd really been hoping that going to camp would change things with my best friend, Em Taylor.

Former best friend.

Temporary former best friend.

We met three years ago at camp.

"You're hogging that tarantula," was the first thing she ever said to me.

Nothing screams zoo camp like tarantulas.

At that point, we were about halfway through the two-week-long Chicagoland Chimp-Champ Zoo Camp. It was held in this circular room with wall-to-wall carpeting way in the back of the zoo. Inspirational animal posters lined the walls. It was creepily like somebody's idea of an artificial habitat zoo enclosure for nine- and ten-year-olds.

I'd thought the Lauras were doing the camp, too, but they apparently changed their minds.

At the Chimp-Champ Zoo Camp, each day had a theme. They were trying to build the excitement, you know, so the first day was "Get to Know Your Phylum" and the last day was "How to Properly Hold a Monkey." At the halfway point, we'd just reached "Predator Day."

Cue the tarantulas.

So aside from me, my tarantula, and the girl with the Indiana Jones whip who was crowding us, there were ten other very loud and excited kids, three other tarantulas, and only one counselor.

Just to recap: four tarantulas total. One counselor.

The tarantula-to-counselor ratio was way off.

If there had been fewer tarantulas and more counselors, *somebody* would have noticed that I'd been stuck holding a tarantula for the last thirty minutes.

"I've held all the other tarantulas and I'm going to hold this one, too," the girl said as she leaned in.

Her name was Em, and she'd carried that Indiana Jones whip around all week, and I wanted to ask if she thought there was a chance the tarantulas were going to get rowdy, but I didn't actually say anything to her, because over the previous twenty-nine minutes, the specific tarantula I was dealing with had slowly wandered over to the edge of the handler's glove I wore, and was currently one billionth of an inch away from stepping directly onto my arm. I wasn't planning on breathing, much less speaking, until it backed the heck up.

The tarantula raised one leg, taunting me.

Over the noise in the room, Em half yelled at me, "I can't compare them if I don't hold them all."

A second tarantula leg went up.

Oh boy.

"It's unscientific if I don't," she said loudly.

A third leg.

"I'm making a chart," she hollered.

The legs twitched.

The tarantula was about to start moving.

Oh help.

"I've been—" But she didn't say any more, because at that moment, three legs still hovering, the tarantula *leaned*, sort of slow-motion *glommed* toward the patch of my arm in front of it, and I straightened my arm with a snap and the tarantula popped into the air, legs scrambling.

That was when the giant owl flew directly between me and Em and ate the tarantula with a loud crunch.

We'd flattened ourselves on the ground, but once we recovered enough to look around, we saw that the bird had perched on the bookcase next to us, parts of the tarantula hanging out of its mouth.

"What did you do?" cried the counselor, Jenny, as she rushed over to me.

"Don't look at *her*," said Em. "*Fovea's* not the one who ate the tarantula."

The entire room turned to watch while the owl finished swallowing.

"Watch closely," Em narrated. "They don't chew their food. They just swallow it and then whatever they can't digest, they'll barf up later in a pellet—"

"Why were you hiding that tarantula?" Jenny was not happy with me. "I clearly announced that we were moving on to the next predator. I collected the tarantulas!"

"I'm sorry," I said, pulling myself back to sitting. "It was so loud. I didn't notice—"

"Terrific. You didn't notice," said the counselor, "and now we're one tarantula short—"

"Wait. Why is it all her fault?" asked Em. "*You* didn't count the tarantulas—and there were only *four*."

"I was thinking about the owl already," Jenny said, but she didn't sound too sure of herself. "I really like the owl."

"And the owl really liked that tarantula," Em said. We all looked at him. His eyes were closed and he looked extremely satisfied. A small piece of leg came unstuck and fell from the owl's beak.

"I'm so sorry," I said again. Partly to Jenny, but mostly to the tarantula.

"Don't you dare apologize!" Em said. She stood to face Jenny. "And you! This is natural selection, and natural selection doesn't care about your plans. If you're going to call it Predator Day, you have to be okay if something eats something else. That is *the definition* of a successful Predator Day."

Jenny stared openmouthed at Em. The rest of the campers started a slow clap. The owl made a noise that I am 99 percent sure was a burp.

Afterwards, while Jenny was putting the owl away, Em leaned over to me and said, "That was amazing. The life cycle in action."

"I still feel bad, though," I said. "And I'm not even a tarantula person."

"Doesn't matter what kind of person you are in the face of the food chain," she said. "Nice people get eaten by lions just as often as mean people do. No big deal."

"I'm not sure I under—"

"And anyway," she added with a wicked smile, "you made that owl's day."

"I guess—"

"*Look* at him."

I wouldn't have guessed that owls could smile. I'd have been wrong, apparently. And Em was right: the happy, peaceful look on the owl's face made me feel better. By the time we all left that afternoon, I completely agreed that it was the tarantula's destiny to get eaten by the owl.

And Em was just getting started. For the rest of the time, she ruled zoo camp with me at her side. She broke into the snack cabinet while I was lookout, and then we ate the heads off the entire carton of animal crackers. She taught the parrot to say "I am not a parrot" while I distracted Jenny with a fake stomachache. Em even led a protest until *all* of the last three days were renamed "How to Properly Hold a Monkey." During her victory speech at the lunch table, I stood behind her with a poster she'd made that said MONKEYS ARE WORTH IT.

On the last day of camp, as Em and I ate cold grilled

cheese sandwiches together under the rain forest mobile, she said, "So, what's next for you?"

"A week of swim camp with the Lauras. If they show up."

"Sounds boring," she said. "*Pottery* camp is where it's at."

My mom and dad made a couple of calls, rearranged my plans, and all of a sudden I was seeing Em every day. For three summers in a row, we hit all the same camps at the same time. At pottery camp the first summer, she made a vase with eight compartments. I made a lot of those coasters. At theater camp the next summer, she played Hamlet. I played the skull. At horse camp last year, she rode horses; I fell off them. It was a perfect summer friendship that became a perfect regular friendship when Em showed up at my school at the beginning of seventh grade. I couldn't believe it.

"My parents separated," she said. "So my mom and I moved to be closer to her work."

"Sorry." I wasn't sure what to say.

She didn't look like she knew either, which was not very Em-like.

We stood in the hall by her new locker, kids pushing past us on either side.

"I am not a parrot?" I finally said.

She smiled. "I am not a parrot."

And instantly school was the best. We'd hang out

afterwards, too. Em's mom was always home by the time school was out, so I started going there in the afternoons. Em came to my house on weekends. It worked out perfectly.

Until Em started spending time with Dana DeLuce.

Suddenly Em didn't think it was so convenient for me to go over to her house.

Back in my own kitchen after school, I'd make toast for myself with the toaster that burned Hippocrates' face on each piece of bread, and tell myself that Dana DeLuce was temporary and that I just needed to try harder. If I tried harder, it would be fine.

But it wasn't. Dana DeLuce was like Em in every way I wasn't—she was sporty and cool and in loads of clubs. The harder I tried, the tighter they got. I kept telling myself that it was only a matter of time before Em realized that she was bored hanging out with somebody so much like herself.

I was wrong.

Dana turned out not to be the boring one.

"Hey, guys!" I wedged myself in line behind Em one morning in early January. She and Dana were talking as our class slowly inched its way down the science hall toward the auditorium. There was some sort of big music assembly that day, and the whole school was on the move. "Hi," I said, again. They didn't even glance back at me.

Try harder.

"Hey," I said one more time, and they actually turned. "If you—both of you—wanted to come over this weekend, my parents might take us somewhere."

"Not the museum again," said Em.

"What's wrong with—"

"Will they take us to their lab?" she asked. Back when she was exclusively my summer friend, I'd told Em all about the lab. And ever since, she'd been determined to check it out. I think it was part of her cycle-of-life appreciation. It was kind of nice to fall into the old routine. She'd ask and, just as predictably, I'd tell her there was no way in a million years.

"There's no way in a million—"

"What lab?" interrupted Dana.

"Oh," I said as we reached the auditorium and headed up the aisle toward our block of seats. "My parents are . . . doctors."

"Not *just* doctors," Em said.

"No—they are totally *just* doctors," I said, hoping that Em was getting my message. "Plain old normal doctors."

We scooted into the row and sat down just in time for Ms. Jacobs, the principal, to come out and start talking into the microphone. She was welcoming us and telling us stuff about the assembly: the orchestra would play, then the band, then the chorus, as a sort of Welcome Back From

Winter Break concert of something something something, but I barely heard any of it. I was only aware of Em on the other side of me whispering to Dana.

"No way," I heard Dana say, and that was pretty much the beginning of the end, because then Dana turned to Devon Kovach and whispered something to *him.*

"What?" Devon said loud enough to make Ms. Peters shush him from the end of the row. He waited a second and then leaned past Dana to ask me, "With dead bodies? Like, your mom and dad have a legit morgue?"

"No!" I whispered down the line. "Not a morgue! They're *doctors.*"

But next to Devon was Kylie, who picked up on the conversation. "Your parents are *morticians*? Like for family time, you embalm people and stuff?"

"Don't morticians drain all the blood out of bodies?" asked Costa on the other side of Kylie.

"Like vampires," agreed Devon.

"*Doctors,*" I whispered again, uselessly.

But the news was spreading. I watched it go, saw it hit the Lauras, who had thought my parents were regular *doctor* doctors since the third grade, and *that* wasn't going to be a great conversation, and Costa had to lean over them to keep it going down the line, and I thought, This isn't happening, how can I stop it, maybe I can fake a heart attack, people do that in movies, or I can freeze time with the superpowers I will discover right now, right now, if I just cross my arms and blink.

I crossed my arms. I blinked. I did not freeze time. I did not have powers.

It was clear what was happening.

I tried too hard. And there was no reversing it.

Out of the corner of my eye, I watched as the awful game of telephone turned the corner, and the whispering jumped from my row to the next row, where the rest of our class was sitting. Beside me, Em watched the assembly, bored, like she didn't have a clue what she'd done. *What exactly had she told Dana?* Did she just mention the lab? Or did she go into detail, like the time she came over for dinner and my mom spent the whole time describing the inside of the spleen she'd operated on that day. Or when my dad talked enthusiastically about the wonders of flash-freezing the recently dead. Or both of them trying to come up with rhymes for "mucus."

I could not stop thinking about all the possibilities.

Finally, the chorus stopped singing whatever song they were singing, and Ms. Jacobs stepped over to the podium again. She adjusted the microphone, cleared her throat, and said only the worst thing she could possibly have said.

She said, "Now, everyone, let's give these folks a hand."

The second the sentence was out of her mouth, the entirely normal sentence *"Let's give these folks a hand,"* somebody in my class started giggling, and within seconds, they were all giggling, and then they were turning and looking directly at me, like they thought I might do something, except I couldn't think of a single thing I was supposed to do. The rest of the school was clapping for the chorus, but MY ENTIRE CLASS was staring at me and giggling wildly.

And then Dana leaned past Em, looking right at me. Her voice was a scalpel cutting through the giggles. "*You* can give them a hand, right?"

A few seats down, I heard Kylie snort, "Just a hand? How about a foot?"

"How about some *eyeballs*?" Costa added.

"It's not like that," I said desperately. "It's not a morgue. They're *doctors*. They work in a *lab*."

"Oh, I get it," said Dana. "They work in a *lab*."

"Yes," I said, grateful. "Yes."

"Yessss, masssster," said Devon, doing a terrible impression from that Frankenstein movie.

And with that, they all lost their minds.

Now that the cat was out of the body bag, I knew how this was going to play out. I couldn't possibly say, *No, wait, it's just my parents. I don't cut up bodies every day. It's those people I live with. They do it.*

It wouldn't matter at all. I was gross by association. Even while they were laughing and yesss-massster-ing, I could see the kids around me pull away, like I was contaminated with cadaver grossness. It was exactly what I'd been afraid would happen if anybody found out.

I closed my eyes and sank into the hard wooden chair and wished that I could keep sinking, out of the auditorium, down past the first floor and the school's basement, through the dirt and the Earth's crust and those other layers and all the way to the other side of the planet, where I could start a new life.

The gravity of humiliation should've totally made that possible.

But it didn't happen. Even with my eyes closed, I knew I was still stuck in the auditorium, because to my left, I heard a sound that made it all heart-smashingly, unignorably real.

Em. Laughing along with the rest of them.

When I finally opened my eyes, I stared hard at the stage. Everything else—every*one* else—blurred and fuzzed until the chorus was the only real thing left in the room, and I'd never seen anything so clearly before. I started clapping for them, like nothing was going on at all, like everything was fine.

I did it. I gave the chorus a hand.

The sharp, tooth-hurting smell of smoke in the classroom shook me out of the memory. An enthusiastic cheer went up and the kids at the "How to Determine Electric Conductors" table started chanting, "Pyro! Pyro! Pyro!"

In the middle of the group, Howe Berger held some sort of plug-in wand and stared at the smoldering ends of Lindsey Weston's previously waist-length hair. Howe and Lindsey looked equally shocked. Ms. Peters actually noticed and snapped into action, throwing her novel down and grabbing at the small fire extinguisher on the wall.

"Pyro! Pyro! Pyro!" The rest of the class was catching on now.

For the briefest moment, I thought to myself—maybe this is what I need. Howe Berger will become The Pyro, and too bad for him, but maybe everybody'll forget about The Igor, and I can get back to being invisible. Was it wrong to want that? I pushed the question out of my mind. Quietly, I joined in. "Pyro. Pyro. Pyro."

But then Lindsey, apparently recovered, grabbed Howe's hand with the wand and held it in the air triumphantly as the chants continued and Ms. Peters sprayed white foam all over the place.

Howe was a freaking hero.

As the chanting died down, Devon held the frog over his head, intestines tumbling down, and yelled, "Igor! Help! The Monster hates fiiiiiiiiiiiiiire!"

Howe was a hero, and I was still Igor.

I scraped the clay from my catapult off the table, vaguely aware of the Lauras. It wasn't my imagination. They'd moved their chairs away from my side of the table.

It was official.

The assembly was the reason I did not technically have any friends whose houses I could stay at for the summer. It was pretty obvious that I was as likely to make a new friend as my parents' cadavers were to get up and start walking around.

3

HIPPOCRATES
DID NOT WISH HE
LIVED IN A YURT

So, the gross stuff is coming. Heads up.

No pun intended.

But also, seriously.

The next day, the first day of what should have been summer vacation, my mom and I set out to walk the six blocks from our building to the lab. My dad had already left, so it was just the two of us, me squinting against the daylight and her trying to walk with hot coffee.

"Darn," my mom said, spilling the coffee while she grabbed a newspaper from one of the sidewalk boxes.

"Oops," she said, sloshing it as she dodged somebody going into the Korean grocery.

"Arg!" she said half a block later as the coffee splattered in front of the old Museum of Holography.

She stopped to shake the coffee out of her bag, and while she was busy, I pressed my forehead against the door of the museum, looking for any signs of movement or change. It was still dark inside, and the sidewalk trash that had piled up in front of the door wasn't exactly encouraging.

The Museum of Holography had been shut down since February. Every day it stayed closed killed me a little more. My parents, on the other hand, didn't even notice until I told them. Holograms aren't really their thing. They prefer things they can cut into or sew up or repair or replace. They get the *science* part of holograms; lasers bounce and make images hover in the air. They just, very cheerfully, don't understand why anybody would care about them. My mom and dad like the solid world.

Once you make a hologram, you pretty much can't do anything to it. It exists and also it doesn't exist, and it's perfect.

From the window, I could see the welcome desk and the edge of the Michael Jordan machine. Farther in, back past the no-longer-jumping Michael Jordan, there were four small rooms that used to be crammed with holograms hovering in glass tubes. The lights were always low, so you could see the images better—the darker the room, the clearer the hologram. My favorite was the banana. There was also the shark and a dinosaur. The head of the Medusa, of course. But the banana was perfect. It was so simple. Using all those lasers, all that complex science, to make something so simple—it was like a cosmic joke.

For me, the Museum of Holography was the best place on earth. It was straight-up magical.

So of course, after Em moved into the city, I took her there.

"This is bonkers," she said, stepping in front of the hologram of Michael Jordan. "They're making us see something that isn't there. It's like being hypnotized." We'd hypnotize ourselves for a whole afternoon, standing next to each other in front of those light waves. The best part of it was not talking, because I knew we were thinking the same thing.

Four months ago, around the time I realized we weren't thinking the same thing anymore, the museum closed. Just flickered out like a laser. The last day I went, right before it closed with no warning, I was alone. I stood in front of the banana and tried to be enough by myself.

A week later, there was a closed-for-good sign on the door. But, I told myself, as long as the machines were still in there, it wasn't permanent. It might reopen someday. It might.

"See anything in there?" asked my mom, holding up a page of something from inside the bag. Half the page was brown and coffee dripped off it.

"I can still see the edge of the Michael Jordan machine."

"Er—is that good?"

"Better than nothing." I kicked away a little of the sidewalk trash as we started walking again. To the lab. Ugh. The lab. I'd managed to forget for a full second. There were about a million other places I'd rather be going. A chewed-gum landfill. A yurt in Siberia. A wild piranha sanctuary.

My mom was in the middle of sucking the coffee out of her sleeve when her phone rang. It was my dad's ring, Janis Joplin singing *Take another little piece of my heart.* For anybody else, that would be romantic. For my parents, it was a suggestion.

"All set?" she said into the phone suspiciously. "Great. Okay, bye!"

I didn't like the way this sounded.

As we closed in on the lab, my mom and I stepped off the curb and into the cool shadow of the train tracks that ran overhead. The train made a loop around the heart of the city, then stretched its veins in all directions, slicing Chicago into wedges. The lab was just along the edge of a slice, so sometimes you could hear the train rumble by when you were inside the lobby. We ducked under the rusty metal stairway that led up to the train platform and crossed the street, the bland-looking front door of the lab directly ahead.

My parents had picked a quiet side street for their lab. They'd chosen an office building that could have been anything, sandwiched between the equally dull-looking offices of an exterminator and a demolition company—the Death Block, I secretly called it.

In the middle of the Death Block, right in front of the lab, stood my dad. He was smiling broadly in front of a sign he'd taped on the door. What previously read DE LEON AND MUNSON now read DE LEON, MUNSON & MUNSON.

They both looked at me expectantly.

"Wow," I said. "That sure is . . . all of our names."

They stood on either side of me, admiring the sign. I could already tell this was going to be a long day. We stepped inside, the usual blast of cold air hitting our faces.

"Stay here," my mom said excitedly. "We'll be right back!" With that, she and my dad disappeared through the blue door behind the front desk.

"No problem," I said to nobody.

A seven-foot-tall portrait of Hippocrates stared down at me.

The Father of Modern Medicine took up one entire wall of the lobby. In the giant painting, Hippocrates is holding a skull and wearing a toga that clearly doesn't fit him. And he

has a huge smile. Like, dimples. It's not the sort of cheerfulness you expect from the Father of Modern Medicine, but you'd have to take that up with my dad, who painted the portrait back when he was in med school.

Aside from Hippocrates and the front desk, there were two uncomfortable waiting-room chairs and a small table between them. Behind one of the uncomfortable chairs, there was a strange, in-the-wall fish tank. The lonesome lab betta fish swam laps, probably wondering what he'd done in his life to deserve being a cadaver lab fish.

He was new. As one of her last acts as receptionist, Whitney convinced my parents to get a real fish and ditch the plastic one they'd had for years.

Unfortunately for the fish, he was named after the Father of Anatomy, the first guy who officially dissected human bodies for science: Herophilus. It's kind of an intense name for a fish. You couldn't blame him for looking a little panicked.

So aside from the panicked fish and the portrait of Hippocrates, the lobby is really a boringly normal setup. You could almost convince yourself you were in a normal doctor's office.

If all the patients weren't dead.

Just then, my parents burst out of the blue door.

"Ta-da!" they said in unison as my dad pulled a doctor's coat from behind his back. It was exactly my size.

"I'm not a doctor," I said.

"Well, we know *that*," my mom said, chuckling.

"I'm a receptionist."

"But we keep the temperature pretty cold in the office," my dad said as he ceremoniously handed the coat over to me. "Because of course we don't want the cadavers to get warm—"

"Dad."

They'd gotten the lab coat stitched over the pocket to say DR. MUNSON, JR. My mom pointed to my dad's coat, which had been altered to read DR. MUNSON, SR. I reluctantly pulled on the coat and sat behind the desk.

"Perfect," my dad said proudly. Then he slid a clipboard across the desk. "These are today's appointments."

My mom smiled. "We'll be in the back, so you'll greet people when they arrive, sign for deliveries, that sort of thing. But sometimes, people without appointments will try to talk their way past you and into the back. The medical-device salespeople, for example, are very sneaky. When you run a cadaver lab, people want to sell you all kinds of things."

"They can be relentless," my dad agreed.

"So if they aren't on that list, they don't get past you. Actually . . ." my mom said, elbowing my dad. "Actually, she's less like a receptionist and more like a *bouncer*."

"Ha!" my dad said, getting misty. "You're our muscle. Our adorable muscle!"

Ugh.

My dad kissed me on the head. "We're going to get to work. You can call the lab phone if you have any questions. Love you!"

"You, too," I said weakly as they headed toward the blue door.

As they opened it and walked through, I could see down the hallway behind it.

Once you go past that blue door, all the obvious and boring stuff goes away. There's a long white hallway. To the left and right are the conference room and my parents' adorable shared office. The hallway itself is decorated, unfortunately, with my dad's framed drawings of human innards.

Straight ahead, at the far end of the Hall of Innards, is a heavy industrial door covered with various signs, all of which essentially say: YOU DON'T WANT TO COME IN HERE. YOU MIGHT THINK YOU WANT TO, BUT YOU'RE WRONG. ALSO, NO OPEN-TOED SHOES.

That was as far as I'd ever been.

But if you walk through that door, *which is a terrible idea*, you will find yourself in Downtown Grossville. They call that room the wet lab. I do not think they could have come up with a more disgusting name. *What* is wet? You immediately want to know. Despite the fact that YOU DON'T WANT TO KNOW.

Contrary to popular opinion at school, I'd never been in there.

Not interested.

Didn't even want to think about it.

Good old cadaver lab.

My home for the entire summer, according to my parents.

I looked up at Hippocrates. I looked over at Herophilus. I glanced at the clipboard.

Okay, I was a bouncer at possibly the worst idea for a club ever.

But still, a bouncer was miles better than being an Igor. Plus, most of the people involved with a cadaver lab aren't going to give you any trouble, *if you know what I mean.*

Then, for the other people, I had a list. Let them come in if they were on the list. Tell them to leave if they weren't.

I mean, I could 100 percent GUARANTEE that there weren't going to be lines of people fighting to get into my cadaver lab. I could do this. Until I found a way to get out of it, I could do this.

The first hour did not exactly fly by.

It would have been a great time to play around on my phone, if I were a person whose parents had let them have a phone, but since my parents were obsessed with studies about brain development and little screens and whatever, I was stuck with a desktop and a desk. So I played around on the computer and opened all the drawers so I could go through Whitney's left-behind stashes of stuff, which turned out to be, in fact, way educational. Probably not how my mom originally envisioned.

First of all, Whitney had the widest variety of tampons I'd ever seen in person.

There was a bottle of bright purple nail polish.

She had apparently saved every sticky note she'd ever written.

There were takeout/delivery menus for practically all the restaurants in the entire city.

And at the very bottom was a crazy elaborate manicure kit, including a bunch of different kinds of scissors, a dozen tiny chemical bottles labeled REMOVE and STRENGTHEN and DISSOLVE, plus some weird-looking tools and what was definitely the biggest, sharpest nail file known to man. Or at least known to me.

Clearly, Whitney had been getting a lot of work done around here.

I decided against giving myself a terrifying-looking manicure, and right around then, four exhausted med students slogged through the front door. I checked off their names and let them go on through the blue door. It swung shut behind them with a click.

Soon after that, a deliveryman dropped by, wearing a shiny blue jumpsuit and matching beret. He smiled. Seemed nice. Friendly.

He set a small package on my desk.

The package had red tape on it, and bright stickers that said REFRIGERATE IMMEDIATELY and BIOHAZARD. My mom had told me about delivery people coming by. She had not said a word about what they might be delivering. All of a sudden it was gruesomely obvious.

The guy adjusted his shiny blue beret.

I guess when you're a shipping company specializing in body parts, you get to dress your people any way you want.

"You new?" he asked.

I nodded.

"Cool. So, probably best to get that in the fridge. You know. Before it thaws." He smiled, got me to sign for the package, and then told me to have a great day as he left. Me alone. With the box.

Inside that box was a body part. Some Body's Part. I tried not to think about what exactly would fit in a box that size. Instead, I dialed the number for the wet lab so someone could come out and get the thing, but nobody picked up. They were busy. Great.

The box and I stared at each other.

After a minute, I scooted the computer monitor between us.

I looked up at Hippocrates, who seemed to think this was hilarious.

After another minute, I went over to the fish tank. The box could have the desk. That was fine.

I was in the middle of hanging out with Herophilus and trying to come up with a new summer plan for the billionth time when my mom swished out to the front in her blue surgical gown and booties.

"Hot dog!" she said, leaping for the little biohazard like it was Christmas. "My bull urethra!"

Her *bull urethra.*

She admired the box. "Why didn't you call? We need to get this baby in the fridge!"

"I did call. You didn't answer."

"Aha! I bet we were in the freezer—we should really get a phone line in there. It's so hard to hear the phone ring when you're neck-deep in necks!" She winked.

I cringed.

"How's it going out here?"

"Oh . . . quiet," I said, which was true. Bull urethras hardly ever said things out loud.

"Don't worry, it gets more exciting!"

"Does it?"

"So much better than you thought, right?" She shook the box for emphasis, like it was a maraca.

"It's definitely . . ."

"A blastula?" She winked again.

I didn't get it, but I was confident that the joke was both medical and revolting. "Sure," I said. "A total blastula."

"Today's been busy," she went on, cheerful and oblivious, "so we're ordering lunch. We'll celebrate your first day!" She held the box up triumphantly. "And the bull urethra!" Then she headed back to the wet lab, even cheerier than before.

The food eventually arrived, filling the lobby and the hallway with the thick smell of barbecue. I locked up, flipped the sign to CLOSED, and everybody gathered in the conference room and started making plates except for one of the students. He stopped at the door, got really pale, and then backed out, saying something about getting a cheese sandwich.

"It's the barbecue, I think," my mom said, when she came back from letting him out the front door.

"The ribs," my dad agreed, nodding as he chewed. "You know, because . . ." With a mouth full of barbecue, he waved toward the lab and suddenly I understood exactly what he meant.

I pushed my plate away from me and sighed. My parents were monsters. Maybe everybody at school was right. Maybe I *was* gross by association.

When my parents and the three remaining students

walked through the lobby about half an hour later, deep in conversation about some kind of hemispheric procedure, I happened to be right in the middle of this computer game where you're in this tree world helping these squirrels—actually, never mind, that makes me sound like a four-year-old. Just take my word for it. It's a freaking hard game. There's all these nuts.

Anyway.

I paused the game and tried to look less like a four-year-old. It worked, somehow, or maybe my parents were anxious to make me feel at home, because they agreed to let me stay by myself for an hour while they went to some lecture on a noninvasive something or other.

My dad and the students waited outside while my mom gave me instructions. "We're not expecting anybody, so it should be quiet. If there are any deliveries, you can accept them. But nobody else comes in. Keep the door locked. If you need us, call us. We'll have our phones. And could you help clean up? Just do a sweep of the conference room so there aren't lunch things left out?"

This was great. If I could prove that I was responsible being left alone for short periods of the day, maybe I could convince them to let me stay at home. The whole me-at-the-lab experiment could be short-lived.

They all left, and I decided to clean up the leftovers from

lunch first. Once that was done, I could get back to the squirrel game. The nuts awaited, you know.

Most of the food in the conference room was already gone, so there wasn't even that much to take care of. I tossed the empty soda cans in a bag for recycling, threw everything else out, and wiped down the table. Done.

I was on my way back out to the lobby when I heard someone talking behind me.

Directly behind me. Coming from *in the lab.*

I stopped right where I was, surrounded by line drawings of nerve endings and ear canals. I must've misheard.

But then the talking happened again, and I jumped, dropping the bag of soda cans; as they clattered all over the floor, I ran into the lobby and slammed the blue door behind me. Superfast, I reviewed in my mind who had left for the lecture: my mom, my dad, the three remaining med students. All of them. Nobody was still back there.

Except somebody was there.

My heart was suddenly beating all over my whole body. My mom would have said that was anatomically impossible. She would have been wrong.

Okay. Maybe there was a mouse. Or something. Something mouselike.

Or maybe it was something worse, like somebody broke in the back way, where the bodies came in.

Or...

My stomach lurched.

Had I locked the door behind my parents? I didn't remember doing it. A robber wouldn't even have had to sneak in. Freaking *anybody* could have waltzed right in while I was cleaning up coleslaw. All right. Possible robbery, possibly my fault, definitely in progress. I needed options.

I could call the police.

And then if it was a false alarm, I'd look like a wuss and my parents would never ever leave me alone again, and I'd be stuck working at the lab and going to surgery lectures until I was an old lady.

I could ignore it.

And then if someone was back there, my parents would get ripped off, all their expensive equipment gone, and it would be my fault.

I could check it out really quickly and then run back into the lobby and lock the door between us.

Then I could call the police if there was a reason to call the police.

Boy, I hoped there wasn't a reason.

I flashed back to a conversation between my parents about surgery, and how if you picture yourself doing a surgery, you'll be better prepared when you do it for real. So I pictured myself being the biggest, baddest bouncer ever.

And then I had one bonus flash of inspiration.

I remembered Whitney's giant nail file.

I ran back to the desk and dug under the menus to pull out the file. I slid off the cover. It looked crazy sharp. This was nuts.

I pictured myself stabbing a robber in the leg so he couldn't chase me. I pictured myself running back to the lobby and locking the blue door and calling the police.

It was probably nothing. But I was prepared.

Or I thought I was.

This is what went down:

With my heart doing its anatomically incorrect thing, I opened the blue door. I carefully stepped around the soda cans I'd left on the floor and stood right in front of the lab door. I could hear a voice on the other side, kind of singing a little, but I couldn't quite hear what the song was. Okay. This was looking up. Maybe it was the radio.

Or else a singing robber. Stab him in the leg, I thought. If you have to stab him, stab him in the leg.

I put my hand on the doorknob, and as I pushed the door open, I heard a new voice singing. *It has to be the radio*, said part of my brain.

Stab them both in the legs, said another part.

And then the door was all the way open and the bright shining white of the lab floors and walls and the metal tabletops blinded me for a second.

I blinked hard.

And I saw that there was going to be no stabbing in legs.

Because the voices were coming from heads.

Two heads.

Heads that did not have legs. Or, in fact, anything below the neck area.

I definitely didn't picture myself throwing up all over the floor.

But I did it very well anyway.

4.

HIPPOCRATES DID NOT BARF WHEN STARTLED

"Oh man, now *I'm* feeling sick," one of the heads said.

"You'll be fine," the other one said.

"I'm going to vomit, Andy. I have that weird taste in my mouth," the first one said. "I can't help it, it's like a natural instinct, I see it, I do it."

"You don't have a stomach," I said, stepping away from the small pool of my barf as it started to roll downhill toward the drain in the middle of the floor.

"Thank you," said the second one. "I've been trying to tell him that for days."

I started to say, "You're welcome," but there were two *heads* looking back at me, and then everything was spinning and my own head felt light, like a balloon floating away, and I turned and walked out, ignoring the voice that called after me, "Wait! Come back! Come back right now!"

I pushed through to the lobby and the door shut behind me. It was quiet again. I laid the nail file on the desk and looked up at Hippocrates.

"Are you playing with me?" I demanded. He just kept smiling.

I closed my eyes. Was my *own* brain playing with me?

Maybe. I'd accidentally just seen into the heart of Grossville. I'd probably seen something so horrible, so completely horrifying, my brain couldn't compute. That was more than enough to make a person hallucinate talking heads. And therefore barf. I mean, I'd barfed for less before. It's not that I'm delicate.

I'm just...let's say...suggestible.

I floated over to Herophilus and leaned my forehead against the cool glass of the tank. I never should have gone into the lab. Nobody goes in the back, my mom had said. But I did, and now I had to do the responsible thing. Obviously, the responsible thing was to completely cover my tracks so that no one would ever know I was there.

I prepared myself for a return visit.

There was a supply closet along the Hall of Innards

where I grabbed some cleaning stuff to take care of the barf. Then I stopped in front of the lab door. I might have hallucinated the talking, but I didn't think I'd hallucinated the heads. I took a deep breath.

This was the impossible part, actually forcing my feet to take me back into the lab. I pushed open the heavy door and took three slow steps forward. I tried to keep my eyes on the ground, but instead, I discovered this interesting fact: sometimes, your body just does whatever it wants. And so my eyes drifted from the barf on the floor up to the table, and whoops—right on top—there were the heads.

Tabletop heads. Like a hologram gone solid. Like a hologram gone wrong.

I couldn't take my eyes off them.

And they stared right back.

They were side by side—similar-looking at first, both of them pinkish-gray and splotchy and potato-y. It was like a magic trick, like a magician had performed some kind of spectacular head removal act and then gotten a call from his grandmother and wandered off and left the heads right where they were, unattached and magically neglected.

The longer I looked, the more I saw past the obvious, *you know*, and noticed how different they were from each other.

One was totally bald with the lightest blue old-man eyes I'd ever seen. The blue was so faint it had faded to almost nothing. He reminded me of the white mouse we'd had in my second grade classroom, the mouse who'd always seemed old, even when we first got him as a baby.

The other head was like a storm cloud, with dark eyes and absolutely colossal dark gray eyebrows that sprigged in every direction and looked so heavy they were threatening to droop all the way to his chin. He had hair on top, a dark gray wispy patch that stuck straight up into a triangle. He also had more neck, so he was taller, and somehow more serious. They sat next to each other on the metal operating table and blinked back at me.

Oh help.

I was not hallucinating.

The tall one smiled.

"Woooooooo," the short one whispered, ghostlike. "Woooooooooo. Just kidding! But it's not polite to stare."

"Sorry," I tried to say, but no sound came out. My voice was curled up inside me, refusing to deal. I heard a drip and looked toward it instinctively, immediately wishing I hadn't. Clearish liquid was running off the edge of the heads' table. It dripped rhythmically three feet down into a red bucket somebody had placed on the floor.

What's that? I thought, or *thought* I thought, except apparently I'd said it out loud, because the tall one said, "What's what?" and I pointed and they both tried to see what I meant, shifting their eyes as far to the left as they could, but apparently it wasn't working, because the tall one said, "Maybe a hint?"

My voice was a croak. "Something's dripping. There. Off the table."

"Oh, that's natural," he said. "We're defrosting."

I closed my eyes really tight, speeding back through time, considering the possibility that maybe there *had* been a robber, and he'd hit me on the head. Totally possible. I opened my eyes.

Nope. Heads.

Two of them.

I dropped the cleaning supplies on the counter next to the doorway and steadied myself against the edge.

"So, I don't mean to sound critical," said the short, mouselike one, "but really, could you do something about that vomit? As I was saying to Andy, I have kind of a sensitive stomach."

"You don't have a stomach!" said the two of us, me and the tall one, at the exact same time.

The short one gasped, offended.

"All right, look," I said, forcing myself to keep talking. "I've seen movies. I know what happens when you ignore the first step of a zombie disaster. It's all downhill from there."

"I don't believe I follow you," said the tall one.

"I shouldn't even be in here," I said. "But I am, and

it would be uncool of me to ignore the beginning of this zombie-head apocalypse or body-snatching situation or whatever it is. So, um, can you please tell me what's going on? What exactly are you doing here?"

"We *told* you."

"Defrosting."

It was time to walk away again.

5.

HIPPOCRATES ABSOLUTELY DID NOT HAVE CONVERSATIONS WITH BODILESS HEADS. HE JUST DIDN'T.

I hadn't gotten an answer about the zombie takeover thing, and I hadn't dealt with the barf. Those were the only two reasons I found myself in the wet lab again a few minutes later, face-to-face-to-face with the two chatty bodiless heads.

"Whitney's replacement, right?" the tall, dark-haired one asked.

"No one is *replaceable*, Andy," said the short, mouse-like one.

"First things first," the tall one said, ignoring the short one. "What's your name?"

Before I could say anything, the short one added, "Ooh, and what's your astrological sign? Your rising sign? Your moon sign?"

"I don't know—"

"YOU DON'T KNOW ANY OF YOUR SIGNS?"

"Also: Are you here all week?" the tall one asked.

"I'm—"

"How about this—do you know your year animal?" The short one was very focused. "Let me guess. Year of the Tiger? Rabbit? I'm getting huge rabbit vibes."

"I really don't—"

"We're very pleased to make your acquaintance," said the tall one.

"What are you doing with that alarmingly big fingernail file?" asked the other.

I'd picked up the file again. How did I not notice that? This was exactly how people accidentally stabbed themselves.

"Alsoooo, just a little reminder about that vomit," said the short one. "It's not going away on its own."

"I'm *working* on it," I said, trying to picture myself not hyperventilating. "I'll be back."

"Fantastic," the tall one said. "Looking forward to it."

The short one started to laugh. "I just tried to nod! Oh, that was weird! Andy, have you tried nodding?"

As I turned to walk out, I saw the tall one roll his eyes.

My dad was always telling me that when a project is overwhelming, you have to break it down into smaller pieces. Then it's doable. This seemed like a good moment to try this out. So first I was going to clean up. Then I was going to talk to the two bodiless heads on the table about whatever they needed to talk about.

Doable.

I dropped the file back into the bottom drawer out front, grabbed a dustpan from the supply closet, and returned to the doorway. The tall one started to talk, but I stopped him. I wasn't ready yet. I pushed the barf into the drain, and then got a bunch of paper towels to wipe up the rest. The heads watched, their eyes following my every move. One of them whistled a tune. They were pretty . . . nonaggressive for zombies.

"Ahem," whispered the short one. "There's a glop there on your right—"

Maybe they were shooting for world domination by being slightly irritating. They were going to slightly irritate humanity into oblivion. It was a possibility. After everything was wiped up, I sprayed the area with lemony disinfectant, which made the tall one sneeze.

"¡Salud!" whispered the short one.

"You don't have to keep whispering," I said as I disinfected the dustpan.

"Sorry," whispered the short one.

The tall one rolled his eyes again.

When there was finally nothing else for me to clean, I washed my hands and stood in front of them again. "So, yes, I'm Whitney's replacement."

"Hmm..." the tall one said, looking at me like he was figuring something out. "Well, I'm Andy Konak and this is Lake Lumino."

"Are you the leader of your people?" I asked Andy Konak.

"I like to believe I am a leader," he said thoughtfully. "So I'll say yes."

"*I'm* the tenor, though," said Lake. "Just so we don't forget." Then he turned his attention to me. "And you are?"

I didn't understand what was happening here, and I definitely wasn't sure why we had to get to know each other. But, whatever. "I'm Fovea Munson," I said weakly.

Andy shot me a familiar, incredulous look. "Your name is *Phobia*?"

"No, 'Fovea.' With an *F.* And a *V.*"

"Sounds like 'Phobia.'"

"Thank you. That will be another great addition to my already really impressive list of nicknames."

"Really, it's *Fovea*?"

I nodded.

"Ah," said Andy Konak's head. "That's a family name?"

I shook my head.

"Um . . . because your mom's from . . . She's from somewhere, right?" asked Lake.

I sighed. This was going just about as well as the beginning of every school year. I was pretty disappointed, frankly—here I was talking to *two supernatural-ish heads* and having the exact same conversation I had every single day of my life. "My name's not Filipino. It's Surgeon. It means 'eyeballs.'" This was all making the afterlife seem a whole lot more predictable than I'd imagined it to be.

"Ah," Andy said again, politely.

At least he didn't laugh, which officially made him nicer than every single person I went to school with. He had that going for him. Too bad not much else seemed to be going for him. I couldn't stop staring, first at one of them, then at the other.

"What—what's wrong? Is my hair messed up?" Lake asked, and then laughed hysterically. "Kidding. Oh, kidding. I know. No hair!"

"No other things, too," I said, realizing as soon as the words were out of my mouth that it probably wasn't a helpful thing to say at all.

"You don't need to rub it in," he said indignantly. "It's no walk in the park, here. I'm eighty percent ghost. LOOK AT ME! ALL OF MY BEST PARTS ARE GHOST!"

"Lake," Andy said, "for heaven's sake, please refrain from elaborating about which parts you consider those to be."

Lake sniffled. "Sorry. I've been having mood swings. It's my stupid limbic system again."

"Your what?" I asked.

"Er . . . you probably don't care to hear about it," Andy said.

"Of course she does!" said Lake. "She cares."

"I . . ." There wasn't a good way out of this.

"See? She cares!"

Andy sighed. "If you insist."

"I got freezer burn," Lake whispered.

"He . . . ah . . . was originally in a freezer at a slightly less upstanding lab."

"Freezer burn on my feelings," Lake whispered again.

Nope. I definitely didn't want to hear about this.

"The other lab missed a few electrical bills and their power was shut down." Andy cleared his throat. "During that time, Lake partially unfroze, and there was some unfortunate positioning."

"I fell sideways."

"So a little more water got into certain sections of his brain, and then when he refroze, those areas expanded, and to cut a potentially very long story short, he has a lot of feelings now. Strong feelings."

"The new me is *exhausting*," Lake said. "But I love it!"

"I see," I said, trying to sound like I saw. I took half a step closer to Lake. "How long—you know? How long have you been . . . a head?"

"Ahead of what? Like, *the curve*?"

I bent down to his level. "Right. Okay, how long have you been . . . here?"

"No clue," he said glumly. "It's really hard to tell in the freezer."

Andy agreed. "He's right. It can be difficult to keep track. But, *speaking* of being out of the freezer, we need a favor now that we're out on the town!"

"You mean out on the table," I said.

"Well, semantics," said Lake breezily.

"Ahem," said Andy. "The important part is actually that we need a favor."

There was a pause in the conversation.

I stood again. "You mean from *me*?"

Andy smiled a mostly toothless smile. It is not cool, in my book, to ask a person for a favor before you've told them whether or not you are a zombie. I said, "Nothing personal, but..." and then I got stuck on it actually being very personal. The fact that they had no bodies seemed very, very personal.

"But what?" asked Lake, like he couldn't think of a single problem with any of this.

"I understand this is a slightly unusual situation," Andy said.

"*Slightly?* This doesn't make sense *at all*," I said, darting around to the back of the operating table, like it might help me figure them out. It didn't, of course. They were heads in the back just as much as they were heads in the front. "Is this like that chicken thing I've heard about, the running-around-with-the-head-cut-off thing?"

"Is she comparing us to chickens?" Lake asked.

"No," I said. "Well, yes, actually. I just want to know if this is *normal*. Like, is it a regular thing that happens to everybody and I just don't know about it? Is this eighth-grade biology stuff?"

"Oooh, it's been such a long time since we were in school, a really long time—" Lake started.

"I think, by the way..." I interrupted him as I made my way back around to the front of the operating table. "There's a monumental flaw in the system if we have to take sex ed *before* we take the class where they tell you that you go on living after your head is cut off. What about, like, Marie Antoinette? That whole getting-her-head-chopped-off thing was no big deal? AND," I said, wheeling around, "what about death in general? Does this mean my Grandma Van will never *actually die*?"

"I, er, don't believe I know her," Andy said.

"So? So *maybe*? How do you figure out something like that for sure?"

"Well . . . it's all a bit iffy," Lake began.

"It's IFFY? Death? IS IFFY?"

"He means it's complicated," Andy jumped in. "Much, it seems, like your relationship with your Grandma Van."

"Yeah. That's—complicated." There was a pause and they glanced at each other. I should have left Grandma Van out of this. "Let's forget I said anything. Next question: Do you talk to everybody?"

"No, but we used to talk to Whitney," Lake said. "Before she—"

Andy coughed.

"Before she what?"

"Oh, left. Before she left."

"And," Andy interrupted, "she was going to do a very important favor for us. Now that she's gone, we need some-one else to help us."

"I bet my parents would be happy to help."

They glanced at each other.

"Your parents, they can't. We have other business with them."

"You have business with my parents?"

Andy cleared his throat. "Mostly we play, you know—"

"Games?"

"Dead," said Andy.

"I like possum better," Lake offered. "Playing possum sounds all-around nicer."

"So they don't know you can talk."

Lake giggled. "They don't expect it, see, so we just close our eyes and keep quiet, and they don't notice a thing. I'm a double threat, you know. Singing, acting. I could dance, too, if I had my legs." He looked off into the distance and sighed dramatically. "Miss those things."

"Bummer about the leg thing, but you should really just ask my parents. For the favor. Really. They're *doctors*. Helping other people is what they're supposed to do. They even took, like, an oath about it."

"No," Andy said sternly. "Your parents' view that we are just a collection of anatomical features needs to stay in place. That's why we donated our bodies to science in the first place. We won't be helpful to science if they're more worried about hurting us or interested in talking to us."

"We do have *a lot* of interesting things to say," Lake added.

"Hold up." I had to steady myself on the counter again. "Does that . . . neck business hurt?"

"No, no," Andy reassured me. "In fact, nothing has hurt since we, you know, became one of the deceased."

"NOT that it's all hunky-dory, mind you," said Lake.

"True, true. There have been a few, erm—"

"Surprises," Lake said darkly.

"Exactly. But overall, this postdeath business has been quite painless. So, thank you for your concern, but as I was saying, we could really use a favor."

I tried to make my brain catch up. They wanted a favor. Right. "Maybe you should try somebody else."

"There *is* no one else, Fovea."

I was already backing out of the room. "You know, they'll be back soon, and I shouldn't even be in here. You didn't see me, okay? The thing is, you guys, you like to play possum and I like to play responsible, direction-following, non-lab-going daughter. Good luck, though, working out the favor thing."

As I walked out, I could hear Andy trying to get me to reconsider, and behind him, from the way back of the lab, where I'd spotted what looked like the walk-in refrigerator, a new, deep voice rang out. It was singing.

"Nobody knows the trouble I've seen..."
I walked faster.

My parents came back pretty soon after that, and congratulated me on holding down the fort, but I wasn't feeling too talkative on account of my raging case of PTSDH (Post-Traumatic Stress from Dead Heads), so I just nodded and let them go on through. I was certain they'd be in the lobby again stat, having discovered that I'd been in the wet lab, that I'd barfed and talked to the heads. It felt inevitable.

After an excruciating twenty seconds of waiting, I pulled out Whitney's purple nail polish and, very slowly, started painting my nails. I only got through two fingers. "Fo!" my dad called out from behind the blue door, and I jerked, swiping purple across my knuckle. This was it. I'd been caught. I braced myself. The two of them spilled out into the lobby. My dad was wearing his blue surgical cap and a headband with a high-powered flashlight on it. My mom was wearing one latex glove. They were both grinning. This wasn't what I was expecting.

"Mom had a great idea," my dad said. "Something you could help us with, when you don't have anything else to do!"

"Before we dig back in," my mom said, pulling off the glove excitedly and tucking it in her pocket. "We wanted to get your brain on the job."

"We've been working really hard," my dad added. "But we're having trouble tying it up."

"Not the bull urethra," I said under my breath. "Please not the bull urethra."

They didn't seem to hear me, because my mom started beatboxing.

And then.

Then my dad began to rap:

"My name is Hippocrates, I come from Kos
I am the inventor of the Hippocratic Oath
I'm known for my wisdom and my smarts and my charm
But most of all I'm known for Do No Harm!"

My mom joined him and together they repeated, *"Do No Harm!"*

That was the first verse. The second verse was about Hippocrates' childhood. The third one was about his schooling. It went on and on and on and I mean *on*, while giant, skull-holding Hippocrates smiled down on all of us cheerfully, just having the time of his life, and I should have been relieved that they weren't upset that I'd been in the lab, but it actually made me madder that I'd had to deal with their dumb sawed-off heads—literally the most horrific office supplies imaginable—and *my parents didn't even notice.*

PTSDH. And they didn't even notice.

All they cared about were terrible jokes. And Hippocrates. I was so sick of Hippocrates and body parts and jokes and mortally embarrassing parental rapping. I wanted to run out of there and go somewhere completely Hippocrates-free, which was, of course, nowhere, since technically I was always going to be partly Hippocratesed myself, since my parents had considerately tagged me the moment I was born, just like all their other *stuff*, all their paintings and soaps and aprons.

By the time they got to the eighth verse of the Hippocrates rap, I couldn't take it anymore. "This doesn't even make sense! How can you do harm to patients WHO ARE DEAD?"

They stopped, right in the middle of a *"Do No Harm."* Hippocrates smiled down at us. My face felt hot.

After a moment, my mom broke the silence, her voice unsure. "Fo, sweetheart, it isn't just about hurting somebody or not hurting them. It's about having ethics. And believing in the skills and knowledge to heal people."

"That," my dad tried to explain, "was what the third through fifth verses were about."

"But *you're not healing people.*"

That got their attention. I wasn't trying to be mean. I was just too afraid to say what I wanted to say, which was, *Whywhywhywhy are you making me do this. I'M NOT LIKE YOU.*

"Maybe we should go ahead and get back to work," my mom said after a moment.

"Yeah," my dad said, drooping a little in his scrubs.

"No, I—"

"It's okay, honey."

My parents can do a lot of things, but they can't lie to save their lives.

"You don't have to like the rap."

"We're just glad you're here."

Then they were gone, and it was just me, Hippocrates, and Herophilus. All of us left to sit and think about what we'd done. I didn't *mean* to hurt their feelings. Maybe. Ugh.

I missed the good old days where I fell off horses all summer.

That was all the thinking I managed, though, because suddenly the front door blew open. Standing with his back against the sunlight was a guy in a black suit. He was the right age to be a student, but he had the wrong look. His suit, first of all: the students wore either blue scrubs or white coats. This guy looked like he was going to a funeral.

A huge bag hung at his side, but he wasn't wearing a beret or a jumpsuit. Not a deliveryman.

Process of elimination: I had a salesman in front of me. I already knew I wasn't interested in whatever he was selling.

"Can I help you?" I asked.

"Well, hello," said the guy. His voice snaked in ahead of him, filling the lobby, and I suddenly wished it wasn't just the two of us in there. He slunk toward me. "Looks like there's been a changing of the guard."

"Can I help you?" I asked again.

"Or not a guard," he continued, looking at me sideways. "No, not a guard at all. Guardlike, maybe. Guardish. A demi-guard, perhaps. So, *can* you?"

I hesitated.

He leaned over the desk and smiled. "Can you help me?"

He was giving me the heebie-jeebies, and I ducked his creepy stare by reaching for the clipboard with the list of acceptable visitors. "What's your name?" I started to ask, but he cut me off, taking the clipboard right out of my hand and laying it down on the desk.

"You see," he said, "I'm looking for Whitney."

6.

HIPPOCRATES DID NOT GET CREEPED OUT BY CREEPS

So apparently, Whitney had a way more exciting life at the lab than I'd ever realized. Between the heads and the creepy dudes it was hard to imagine why she'd ever want to leave the job.

"Inko Fredrickson," the man said, stalking across the lobby to rap his knuckles on Herophilus's tank a few times. Herophilus scrammed into his fish castle. I'd have gone in there, too, if I could. "Inko Fredrickson of Fredrickson and Son, Crematorium Express. I'm the son." He raised his eyebrows at me, and did a little magician thing with his hand. "'*We Burn It, Then We Urn It.*' That's our slogan. It also references our fiscal responsibility, you see. *Earn, Urn.* Homophones. Yes indeed, we've ended every year in the black, hmm." He smoothed down one eyebrow.

"A cremator," I said.

He smoothed down the other eyebrow in agreement.

"You burn up . . . people."

An ooky smile spread across his face. "We simply help the deceased along their way. People, pets, whatever you got."

"Pets?"

"Fired up an alligator once." As he spoke, he gazed over at Hippocrates. I couldn't tell whether he was admiring the portrait or working out how much energy it would take to chop a seven-foot-tall man into steaks. I was guessing steaks, because he didn't really seem like a Do No Harm kind of dude. A *cremator.* That was definitely worse than my parents. I'd have wondered what led him down that particular career path, except that he looked like he was born to be a cremator.

And I figured a cremator looking for somebody could only mean bad news. "Did Whitney have a death in the family?"

"No." He turned from the painting and sat on the edge of the desk, flipping the back end of his dark coat at the last minute so he wouldn't sit on it. Settled, he looked down at

me. "No death in the family. But it is exactly that serious."
He very slowly put a hand over his heart.

"Should I call for a doctor—"

"No! Don't call them. Just Whitney." He was definitely
starting to get irritated.

"But Whitney's not here anymore. She quit."

"Oh?" he said, startled. His hand hovered, like he wasn't
sure what to do with it anymore. "Is that so?"

"It's so."

"Perhaps she's going to drop in today."

"I don't think so," I said. "She's in Florida. With her
boyfriend."

He looked shaken and half snorted, "Impossible!" Then,
instead of leaving, he informed me that I must have made
an error. I said I was pretty sure not, but he wasn't even
seeing me anymore. He walked over to one of the chairs,
tapping absentmindedly on Herophilus's tank as he went.
He sat down. And there he stayed.

I was supposed to be a bouncer, but I didn't know how
to bounce that.

I mean, I *tried*.

"Well, too bad," I said. "About Whitney not being here."

"Probably a waste of time for you to stay," I said.

"Did you need her phone number?" I said.

"Somebody should really feed that fish," I said. "Am I
right?"

"Is there anything else you wanted?" I said.

"No!" He twisted to face me. "Whitney will show up. She will. She would not have simply left town without informing me. She is quite in love with me."

"Are you sure?" I asked before I could help myself.

"I have the evidence right here. See?" he said, reaching into the too-big bag and pulling out a fistful of folded papers. "Love letters."

"She wrote those?"

"No, I did," he said, stuffing them back in the bag.

"I'm not sure that's the kind of evidence that proves—"

"Enough!" He stormed out of the lobby onto the sidewalk, and I watched through the window as he made a phone call. I was hoping that would be the end of him, but then he stomped back in, flopped into a chair, stared off at nothing, and started sniffling loudly.

I slouched down and played *Nut Commander* on mute, hoping he would just leave on his own. Probably all bouncers gave up once in a while. I wasn't interested in getting between Whitney and any of her possible boyfriends. Especially this kind. The burning-people-up kind.

Eventually he did leave, right around the time that my mom called. Right after she called, actually. If he'd left before she called, this would be a completely different story.

At the time, I was in the middle of a bonus round. Variety Nut Skee-Ball. I was scoring big, but the cremator in the room was a real buzzkill. And then I heard this bleeping coming from the phone on the desk. I answered and barely heard my mom say, "How's our favorite cellular mass?" The speaker phone made her sound miles away. "Hello? Fovea?" she said.

"I'm here." I tried to find the button that controlled volume. I pushed one that had a bunch of circles on it, and the phone made an angry honk.

"Everything okay out there?"

"Uh-huh." No need to tell them about Inko Fredrickson, still sitting five feet away from me, and how I wasn't even cut out for the simplest thing they could find for me to do.

I kept pushing the buttons.

"We, uh, probably won't be that available for the rest of the afternoon; we've hit a bit of a snag."

"Uh-huh." A snag. Or else they just didn't want to see my face. I glanced at Inko Fredrickson as I hit a couple of buttons, one of which made *my* phone go all speakerphone, so that Inko and I could *both* now hear my mom's voice as it projected out into the whole lobby loud and clear. Back back back. Which button would take it back to normal phone?

"...still on for dinner at Grandma Van's, so we can reheat some of that frozen chicken adobo..." She spoke louder as she walked away from the phone, and, as I tried another few buttons, I could hear my dad yelling from even farther away, "I've officially looked everywhere! It's definitely not in the freezer!" Then my mom again, saying, "How could a specimen just disappear—"

Finally, I did the first useful thing I'd done the whole day. I hung up. They probably didn't even notice. They hadn't been talking to me at that point, anyway, and I really, really hoped all that didn't mean they were keeping chicken adobo in the body freezer. Or, possibly worse, that they'd *lost* a chicken adobo in the body freezer.

I looked up to see Inko Fredrickson staring at me, his mouth open. Without another word, he shut his mouth and took off. I was so relieved to see him go, I didn't even wonder why he left. Instead, I was remembering how I'd thought for a minute that this might be a peaceful job. Right. Nothing was peaceful here. Not even the freaking cadavers.

I went back to the game, but my heart wasn't in it. I kept glancing up to make sure the cremator wasn't coming back in, which is probably how I accidentally clicked on the calendar. A reminder window immediately opened, beeping at me:

 **PRACTICUM:** Thoracic Cavity (thawed)

It took me a second to realize what I was looking at— this was part of Whitney's schedule for the lab. Complete with pop-up reminders. Based on what my dad had said earlier about the ribs, I was pretty sure that was the lab my parents had done that morning before the barbecue lunch. Gross. I closed the window. The computer beeped as another one immediately popped up.

 **DELIVERY:** Bull Urethra (frozen)

Like I needed to be reminded. I closed that reminder window, and it beeped again instantly. There was another one.

 **INTO FREEZER:** Bull Urethra

I closed it quickly, hoping they'd stop, but *another* reminder appeared, and I switched off the monitor before I could read it. Whitney needed to learn how to space out reminders, and I seriously did *not* need a play-by-play of what the bull urethra was up to.

 **MAKING FRIENDS:** Bull Urethra

 **HAVING A GREAT AFTERNOON:** Bull Urethra

 **GETTING DISSECTED:** Bull Urethra

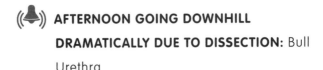

AFTERNOON GOING DOWNHILL DRAMATICALLY DUE TO DISSECTION: Bull Urethra

SINGING EIGHTIES SONGS ABOUT LONELINESS: Bull Urethra

I didn't want to know.

And I didn't *need* to know either. Keeping track of the bull urethra's busy day was not receptionist stuff. Or even bouncer stuff. It was straight-up Igor business. Whitney might have enjoyed keeping track of the schedule, but I was drawing a line. Tomorrow I'd turn off the reminders. Right now, though, I was just trying to get through the day without messing up any more than I already had.

Which was getting harder and harder every second.

My dad came out from the back about an hour later. He was not humming. "You doing okay out here? Need anything?"

"No, I'm fine," I said miserably.

He held up a file folder. "We're still dealing with a minor problem back there, but every Monday, Whitney orders— well, ordered—whatever supplies we need to restock. We thought maybe you could do it, since you're such a computer whiz? You just look at the form, which gives you the web-site and the account number and password. For example, let's go to the site We Love Gloves: Hand Coverings for All Your Needs."

I clicked the monitor back on and pulled up the site my dad was talking about.

"We log in like so . . ."

As we leaned in together, I wanted to say I was sorry for what I'd said earlier, but I didn't think that would fix anything. Being at the lab wasn't making my parents and me closer. It was just emphasizing how much I didn't belong with them.

He went on. "Now that I'm into our account on the site, I just look at the order form in the folder." We studied the form, which was, in fact, pretty self-explanatory. Then we turned back to the computer screen. "You click here to order two boxes of small gloves, here for three boxes of medium, and here for three boxes of large. Make sense?"

I nodded.

For a moment, he hovered like he wanted to say something, but then he just said, "Great. Thanks a bunch, kiddo." He kissed me on the head and walked back through the blue door, silently.

I put the folder aside. Whatever else was inside could wait. I had to come up with a way to get out of this job. If things kept going the way they were going, within a couple of days I was going to be kicked out of this family. First Em. Then the Lauras. Now for some reason I couldn't stop making things worse with my parents. I was seriously running out of things to be kicked out of.

I closed the window for the glove website, and discovered that the schedule-reminder pop-up was still there. I read it before I remembered that I was ignoring it:

 **OUT OF FREEZER:** Heads (2.5 days to thaw)

At least they hadn't been lying to me. They really were defrosting.

And, I realized, I didn't want to be around when they were done. If they were already that gross and irritating half frozen, I didn't want to be anywhere near them when they'd finished the job.

Somehow, I'd find a new summer plan before those guys thawed.

The last thing I needed that night was Grandma Van.

So of course, there we were: my mom, my dad, and I, making our usual dinnertime trek into the maroon velvet lobby of the Swan Song Retirement Village apartment building.

The Swan Song is six blocks from the building we live in, meaning that we spend way too much time over there. It's an old-fashioned place, and has both pros and cons. The really nice part is that it's on the lake, so there are beautiful views. The bummer part is that over every window is a cement demon-swan emerging from the brick and stuck in midflight, so every time you look out of a window at the great view, your first thought is that something terrifying is about to crash in through the glass at you. It's even creepier from outside, like the whole building is going to dissolve into those swans and they're probably going to peck you to death or, if you're lucky, smother you quickly with their icky cement feathers. Those blank cement eyes are the worst.

The ownership really embraced it, though, apparently making sure there were as many demon-swans on the inside as there were on the outside. The indoor ones were wall-to-wall and upholstered, from the giant gray swan frowning in the middle of the maroon lobby carpeting to the nightmare-y inch-size versions on the velvety maroon drapes and the decorative armchairs. Everything matched in the most horrific of ways.

It was the perfect building for Grandma Van.

She lived on the eighth floor, so we hopped on the ancient elevator and rode up slowly. It was cramped in there, even with just the three of us, and the walls were plastered with notices of events going on in the Swan Song. As the flyers indicated, every single club, game night, and singing group had been organized by Julia Klinger, who was, inconveniently, my grandmother's archnemesis. She lived one floor up, and though I'd never met her, she was apparently out to get Grandma Van. My grandmother used to be the boss of the Filipino part of the nursing home, and Julia ran the Armenian part. Ever since Julia took over the social calendar for the entire building, Grandma Van refused to do anything even remotely social, including eat with the other old people, which was why we'd been having dinner there every other night for the last five weeks.

The elevator binged and we walked down the long hallway to her door. It was the one with the enormous portrait of Henry VIII on it. "A man who knew what he wanted," Grandma Van always said admiringly. Like her hero, my grandmother knew what she wanted. Almost every one of our dinnertime conversations revolved around how much Grandma Van looked forward to her imminent demise. She'd planned out her funeral about a million different ways, and every time it changed, she'd tell me my new role.

"You'll lead a procession holding a lit candle shaped like my face. . . ."

"It'll be a cocktail party, and you'll be walking around with my ashes on top of an upside-down pineapple cake. . . ."

"I've rented a flock of swans from the wildlife center. It'll be my tribute to the Swan Song. You can herd swans, right?"

I lived in fear of her death, and it didn't help that according to her, it might happen any moment.

We reached Henry VIII, who snarled at us. My mom

knocked, and after a minute, we heard the electric hum of the scooter moving closer to the door. A few locks turned and the door opened several inches.

A single eye magnified by a pair of drugstore eyeglasses peered out suspiciously. The eyeglasses just barely fought off a mountain of thick purple-black hair that threatened to crush them. Grandma Van did the dye job herself. "Who are you people?"

My dad sighed and shifted the dish of chicken adobo to the other hand.

"Just kidding," Grandma Van said. Her gravelly voice was exactly how I imagined all the concrete swans sounded when they discussed who they were going to swarm first. She grunted, swanlike, and looked past me. "No new friends yet, huh?"

Flap flap flap.

I shrugged, wishing I'd never brought Em over. It had only been like three times, but that was enough. Grandma Van knew where your weak spots were. It was her gift, along with funeral planning.

She turned back to my parents. "What'd you bring?"

My dad peeled back the aluminum foil.

"Chicken adobo. What a surprise." Then, keeping a disappointed eye on us, she hit reverse on her scooter, backing up all the way into her apartment. There was a wire basket attached to the front where she normally kept her enormous purse and a box of crackers, and it scraped a long, ugly line in the plaster of the wall as she went. When she'd gone as far back as she could, she turned the motorized chair and drove into the living room, leaving a few crumbles of plaster in her wake. From around the corner, we heard her say, "Kicking the bucket never looked so good."

Nobody said much over dinner. My parents tried to fake some cheerfulness, but it wasn't very convincing.

"Fovea had her first shift at the lab!"

"Tell your grandmother all about it, Fo!"

Grandma Van sighed deeply and helped herself to some chicken.

There was nothing I wanted to tell anyone about my day, least of all Grandma Van, whose depression might actually get depressed if I mentioned that death was "iffy."

"There's a real fish now," I said. "He spent a lot of time in the castle today." I scooped some chicken for myself and then examined it, remembering the possibility that it had spent some time in the body freezer. I mushed it with my fork. It looked normal, but if I was going to eat it, I needed to be certain. "Where did this come from?"

"Oh—I made it," my dad said distractedly.

Grandma Van sighed again. "Pretending to be Filipino does not fool the chicken," she muttered.

"I helped a little," said my mom.

Grandma Van eyed her. "Helped? You can't even make ice water."

"Dad?" I said. "After you made the chicken, since then, where has the chicken been living?"

"In the freezer," he said, frowning.

"The *kitchen* freezer?"

"As opposed to?"

All right. I was convinced. "Never mind. Please pass the pepper."

There was a pause.

"Speaking of pepper," said Grandma Van, "did you people know that Julia petitioned the management to replace all the pepper grinders with *shakers*? So now instead of twisting the knob to get your pepper, you just dump the stuff on your plate. It's like she's rewarding everybody who has arthritis. Nobody works for anything around here anymore. When I go belly-up, I'm leaving money to this place, but only on the condition that they go back to grinders."

On the way out after dinner, my mom gave Grandma Van a hug.

"Maybe you should try something new, Mom," she said. "Maybe you've been holed up here too long, you know? Maybe you'd like an activity?"

"Bite your tongue!" my grandmother snapped back. "As long as Julia's running things, I am activity AWOL."

"Even, like, bingo?"

A look from my grandmother could kill a cockroach from eight feet away. "I'll be joining the majority soon enough," she said. "Soon enough."

We were all silent.

"That means I'll be dead, babies."

7.

HIPPOCRATES
DID NOT HAVE
ISSUES WITH BEING
LEFT ALONE

Tuesday morning.

My alarm clock went off at six, but I was already awake. I hadn't slept well.

Sure, everything I thought I knew about life and death had been turned on its head, like, literally. But I was actually more stressed out about my parents. They still seemed upset with me and I didn't know how to make it right.

As we left the apartment building, they walked a few

steps ahead of me, talking quietly. They talked quietly, past the Museum of Holography, down the block, and under the train tracks. They never acted like this. It was unsettling, all the way to the lab.

My parents went into the back with no fanfare. I sat down and gave Hippocrates a wave. After yesterday's craziness, it was *too* quiet, so I was actually relieved when they came out again not much later. I shouldn't have been.

"Fo, we...erm...need to step out," my dad said, absentmindedly scratching between his shoulder blades with a long pair of clamp things. "You were a pro yesterday when we were at the lecture hall, so we're going to let you stick around here again, okay?"

"It's not usually like this," my mom said, looking a little worried. "The two of us being gone so much. Normally, there's just a lecture here or there. But we've hit a bit of a—"

"Problem," said my dad.

"Right," said my mom. "A problem. And we need to track a few people down."

"Maybe you could call them? Or I could call them?" I offered.

They shared a glance. "Thanks, Fo," my mom said carefully. "But considering the situation, we need to talk to them face-to-face."

"Maybe I could come with you?" I tried not to sound too desperate.

"Lock the door behind us," my mom said, like she hadn't even heard me. "And you've got the computer, that'll be fun. If you want something else to do, you could feed Herophilus, maybe? Or organize the office supplies? And we'll see you in a bit?"

Everything about this was weird. The fact that I'd had to beg to be left alone yesterday, and now they didn't seem to care at all. Something was wrong.

Now I didn't want to be left.

"See you later," I said. They walked out, waved distractedly through the glass, and were gone. Not a single stupid anatomy joke.

I locked the door, double checked it, and then wandered over to Herophilus. He was doing a pretty bad job of hiding behind some fake seaweed. I wondered how, exactly, I was supposed to feed him since the tank seemed to be part of the wall. I pressed my face against the cool glass, peering through the seaweed into the darkness on the other side of the tank. Where did it go? There had to be a back entrance.

I stuck my head through the blue door and looked down the Hall of Innards. The wet lab was closed. With no heads roaming around, I was a little more confident investigating the conference room, which I'd spent almost no time in, unless you counted lunch the day before.

I flipped on the lights. Nothing had changed. It was

pretty boring—the conference table and matching chairs took up most of the space—but there was a large closet at one end of the room. I opened it and discovered a few lonely lab coats hanging in a corner and, more importantly, the back of the tank, glowing in the dim light. Through the seaweed I could see the empty lobby. Spooky.

From the closet side, you could easily take off the lid and add food or whatever you needed to do. A can of fish food sat on the shelf holding the tank, so I popped off the lid and dropped a pinch into the water. Herophilus swam to the top immediately, scarfing the food like he'd never been fed before in his life. "You're welcome," I said. "I definitely won't be here long, but until I leave, I will hook you up with all the shrimp flakes your fish heart desires." Seemed borderline cannibalistic to me, but he was enjoying it.

Returning to my station in the lobby, I sat down to organize the desk drawers. After that, I'd do that stuff in the folder my dad had given me the day before. I was going to be so productive even *I'd* be impressed with me.

I pulled open the top drawer.

Right.

Lots and lots of tampons.

I didn't know how to organize those things.

I skipped down one drawer. Whitney's collection of old sticky notes. I grabbed a handful, figuring I'd skim through them, make sure they didn't look important, and

THE MORTIFICATION OF FOVEA MUNSON

then throw them out. I read the first one, and immediately discovered a problem. I was pretty sure it was a love poem. More or less.

You're the sauce to my spaghetti,
I'm the footprint to your Yeti.

There were tons of them, just like that one. I didn't know what to do with weird love poems any more than I knew what to do with tampons.

Drawers: 2. Fovea: 0

Next drawer: menus. Finally. That was a good one. First, I'd throw out all the barbecue ones. I dropped a stack on the desk in front of me with a hard *clunk*. Interesting. I sifted through them and pulled out a phone. Whitney's phone. I knew because it looked like the kind of phone Whitney would have had.

Also, it said WHITNEY all across the back of it in rhinestone letters.

She'd left town pretty quickly—overnight, almost. She must've forgotten it. I turned the phone over in my hand. It was either off or dead.

I was getting an idea.

The thing was—maybe I could find contact info for Dean, that boyfriend she mentioned in the note she left my parents. A quick call to him, and I could reunite Whitney with her phone. She'd be super grateful and it would be the perfect moment for me to convince her to move back to

Chicago and her old life. My parents would be so impressed with my new take-charge attitude and how I got their receptionist back they'd let me stay at home the rest of the summer.

I tried the power and the phone jumped to life, a blurry picture of a cat filling the screen. It wasn't locked, so I opened her contacts. They were organized by last name, and of course I didn't know Dean's last name, so I just went through the whole list. Twice.

There was no Dean.

You don't run away to another state with somebody who isn't even in your phone.

Right then, the phone started buzzing all over the place as the messages loaded from all the time it'd been off. Six voice-mail messages. I put it down on the desk in front of me, debating. It wouldn't be wrong to check out the messages if they helped me return the phone to her. Probably?

The first message was from two weeks ago, right around the time she left.

There was a beep. "Whitney," a voice said. "It is I, your Prince Charming! Call me! But don't call me late for dinner, hmm?"

I didn't know what Dean sounded like, but I knew that wasn't him. *That* voice, without a doubt, belonged to a certain cremator who liked to slink around and be all kinds of in-your-face unnerving. Inko Fredrickson hadn't needed

Whitney's number because he already had it. I kept going. The second message was also Inko Fredrickson. And the third.

Beep. "Whitney. You said you liked poetry, so feast your ears on this: 'Ode to a Heart That Beats for Love Despite Having Been Burned to a Crisp: Tha-thump, sizzle. Tha-thump, sizzle. Love. Burns. Forever.' I'm a regular—what do they call them? Lariat? No, that's a cowboy necklace. Laureate. Yeah. Laureate. At . . . your . . . service."

Beep. "Whitney. I know it's early, but I was thinking about adoption."

Beep. "Whitney? Call me! Call me anything, even late for dinner, heh, hmm. Just call me back. Are you actually listening to my messages? I've written them all down in case you'd rather read them. Let me know."

Yeesh. I was glad to not be in the middle of that anymore. I let the voice mail keep playing, still hoping for Dean. The next message was from yesterday.

Beep. "Whitney. I'm standing outside the lab." Oh man. He'd called her while he was here. It made me feel kind of weird for my past self. Also weird for my current self. I was starting to regret my decision to listen to the messages, but now that I'd gotten this far, I didn't feel like I could stop.

It got worse as the message went on. "I thought you loved me. All those things you said about love and growing old together. About cuddling. Staying cozy on cold winter nights. And now you've left me for somebody else? Some *Floridian*? Unbelievable. Unconscionable. Unimaginable. I hereby challenge him to a duel. Now I'm going back in, where it smells like you."

Beep. "Whitney." The last message, from a few hours later. "Just in case you two need some incentive to return from your Floridian paradise so that the duel can commence, I happen to have an incentive right here. As I waited in the lab for you to appear, my tortured heart scabbing over every second, I used my acute sense of observation to determine that your precious lab has lost a specimen. That specimen could be anywhere, Whitney, and as you know, a missing specimen is a MASSIVE BIOHAZARD. Exactly the sort of thing that the state regulatory board would shut a lab down for. Send people to jail for. And if they discover, through an anonymous tip, for example, that there has been a cover-up? Well. I expect the punishment would be very, very harsh.

"I'm giving you *forty-eight hours*. Forty-eight hours to get back here and let me fight for your love. If you start driving now, you'll make it. If you delay, then I'm calling in that anonymous tip and people will get hurt. People that I think you care about.

"I won't let you go without a fight. Good-bye."

I dropped the phone on the desk in front of me.

That lovesick cremator was using my parents as bait.

And I'd given him the hook to stick them on. My stomach turned upside down. A missing specimen. That was what they'd been talking about when I'd put them on speaker-phone. This was my fault. A wolf had come into the hen-house and I'd given him the matches to burn the place down.

Some bouncer.

Some daughter.

I could picture it hanging over my head, like in a spider-web: SOME DAUGHTER. Except instead of cheering, everybody would look at me and shake their heads and say, "Too bad she's not a pig. At least you can eat those after they destroy your life."

I forced myself to breathe.

There had to be something.

Whitney wasn't coming back. Sure, she might have tried to help if she'd heard the messages, but the phone had been in that drawer when Inko called—Whitney'd never heard any of them.

The idea of telling my parents what I'd done made me sick, but if I didn't, then it was up to them to accidentally save themselves. And since the message was from yesterday, they only had one day left. Twenty-four hours to find the thing. The specimen. Or else he would ruin them.

Jail. And even worse, in a way, losing the lab. That's what would really ruin them. My parents without their work—it was impossible to imagine. It was what defined them. It was how they defined the world. It was how they defined me, even. I couldn't let it happen. I had to tell them.

Or.

Or I could find it myself.

I could ask somebody who could tell me exactly where it was.

I walked down the Hall of Innards and toward the lab. I hesitated for just a second outside the door, and then stepped in. They were still right there, on the table.

Except now there was a new guy, just on the other side of Andy.

Three. There were three now. Oh help.

8

HIPPOCRATES DID NOT NEED HELP. HE DID NOT NEED IT REALLY REALLY BADLY.

The third head was on the end next to Andy, looking a lot more frozen than the other guys. That wasn't slowing him down, though.

"And then *I* said, 'Maybe I should get out of this grave-yard, buddy, and then we can have a man-to-man conversation about where my strikes are landing.' And *he* said—"

"Fovea!" cried Lake. "Look, everybody in the whole lab, it's Fovea!"

"There are only three of us," said the new head, looking ticked off. "And we can't really look anywhere else. *And* you interrupted me."

Lake winked at me. "I'm not that into bowling. What do *you* think about bowling, Fovea?"

"Bowling?" I asked.

"Bowling!" bellowed the new guy.

"I can see how bowling might not be a great hobby for right now," I said slowly, trying to appear calm. "Also, by the way, just as I was coming in, you mentioned graveyards? Is that something I should be kept in the loop about?" My fears of a zombie-head apocalypse returned, my mind filling with images of terrifying graspy hands pushing through dirt and reaching out of graves, that kind of thing. Except minus the terrifying graspy hands. How would they get out? Well, I thought optimistically, at least this was going to be a short zombie apocalypse.

"That graveyard stuff was a bowling story," said Lake.

"Only *the* bowling story," said the new guy.

"Of course." I stared at the three of them. I hoped they didn't keep multiplying. Andy and Lake were looking more relaxed than ever, which I figured must be the upside to the defrosting process. The downside: they were getting mushy around the neck. This new guy had an icicle hanging off his chin, and a lot of slightly damp curly gray hair. He took the moment to puff some of the hair out of his face.

"I'm Fovea," I said.

"Hey," he said. "I've heard about you."

"That's super great," I said, giving the other two a stink eye, "because I hadn't heard about you."

The new guy harrumphed. "How about that. Who cares about Old Man McMullen? Been in that freezer longer than either of these two clowns. But who remembers that? Nobody. So, you *do* bowl or you *don't* bowl?"

"No, sorry," I said. "I don't. Especially not in graveyards."

"McMullen wasn't talking about a real graveyard. It's like a bad bowling lane or something," Lake explained, then dropped his voice to a whisper. "Very juju."

"There is nothing juju about it!" roared McMullen. "Juju is for fortune-tellers and crystal sniffers! I'm talking about red-blooded physics!"

"Well, anyway," Lake continued cheerfully, "it's great to see you again!"

"Um, you, too," I said, hoping all this small talk would butter them up. Make them more likely to help me.

"By the way, I've been thinking you're probably a Sagittarius," said Lake. "The archer!"

"Why?" I asked.

"The way you were holding that mop."

"Baloney," McMullen muttered.

"Thanks, um, for thinking of me. Anyway, I was wondering," I said, as normally as I could, "if you guys could help me out with something?"

"What about *our* favor, Fovea?" Andy said. "The one from yesterday?"

They all looked at me. I looked back at them. Right. Their favor. Life was coming at me so hard that what with the blackmail and the decapitations, I'd completely forgotten about *their* favor. I was the only one who could help them, they'd said. And now they were the only ones who could help me. We were all kind of scraping the bottom of the barrel, as far as help went.

"I'll do it," I said. Then I thought of Em. And the Lauras. And the rest of seventh grade. "But I am NOT your Igor."

"You're not our what, now?" asked Andy.

"No bringing you your elbows or something, just because you miss them. No body reassembling. And I probably can't, you know, figure out who killed you or whatever."

Lake laughed, "Oh, honey, nobody killed me." He stopped abruptly. "Unless."

"Nobody killed you, Lake," Andy said. "Natural causes, natural causes. You're absolutely fine."

"Fine? That's a load of tuna," McMullen muttered.

"And you'll help me?" I asked.

Andy smiled. "We'll do anything we can—"

"WHICH IS REALLY NOT SAYING MUCH," McMullen pointed out loudly.

"He's having trouble adjusting to the transition out of the freezer," whispered Lake.

"I can HEAR you. No ice in my ears," said McMullen. "Well, maybe a *little*."

"The thing I need is simple," I said. "I'm trying to find something that's missing." I glanced around at the spotless counters, the smudge-free silver metal operating tables, the organized-to-oblivion shelves. How could anybody lose anything here? "It's a specimen. I don't know what it's a specimen *of*, just that it's not where it should be. So I need to know if you noticed a specimen of something that somebody might have accidentally thrown out or put in a wrong cabinet in the last couple of days."

Suddenly each head was looking off in a different direction. For no reason at all. It was the fishiest thing I'd ever seen.

They knew.

"Where is it?" I asked, feeling the edge in my voice. "*What* is it?"

There was another pause and then Andy cleared his throat. "To begin with, speaking scientifically, erm—"

"*We're* specimens!" Lake said. "There's no shame in it. I'm an *excellent* specimen." He winked at me.

"Thank you, Lake," Andy said. "I was getting there."

My brain was working in slow motion. "So . . ."

"Yes, we know about the specimen that's missing, and what's more, we know where he went."

"He?"

"Right," said Andy. "There should be four of us."

9

HIPPOCRATES
DID NOT MAKE
TERRIBLE DEALS

Of course.

((🔔)) **OUT OF FREEZER:** Heads (2.5 days to thaw)

My parents had LOST AN ENTIRE HEAD. No wonder they weren't themselves. And Inko had actually been right. I didn't know much about what made something a biohazard, except that you were supposed to stay away from those sorts of things, and a random loose drippy head just rolling around somewhere? MASSIVE BIOHAZARD.

A quick look around confirmed that there weren't many places in the lab where a head could roll off and hide.

"Where is it?" Metal counters ran along the walls of the lab, and there was tons of storage underneath. I tried one cabinet after another, but every one of them was full of boxes. Small boxes. Large boxes. No heads.

"He," Lake corrected me.

"Okay," I said, trying the cabinets on the far wall. "Where is *he*?"

"We'll tell you," Andy said slowly, "after you do our favor."

"Why don't we all do our favors at the same time?" I asked as I opened a door toward the back. Nothing but boxes of gauze, stacked high. It was the last place to look, aside from the body part freezer, and I wasn't setting foot in there. I shut it and returned to my usual spot in front of the operating table.

Andy cleared his throat. "You weren't going to come back, were you?"

"What?"

"It was fairly obvious."

"No, come on, you're so ... hard to forget," I said.

"I didn't say that you forgot us, I said you weren't coming back. It's true, isn't it?" I heard Lake gasp, and then Andy continued, "Except then you needed something from *us*."

I didn't figure I needed to say anything. I could feel how guilty my face looked.

"And see, we don't have much leverage around here. We can't go on strike. Can't just walk out."

"Could you just go ahead and tell me where it is if I promise to do the favor? If I cross my heart a million times?"

"Hearts: not actually that reliable," said McMullen. "Where's mine? Who knows? Detroit?"

"Hearts are not the issue," said Andy.

"Hearts are always the issue!" cried Lake.

"*The issue is*"—Andy took control again—"that we just can't risk it. But as soon as it's over, we'll tell you what you need to know."

Lake blinked his blue eyes and smiled.

McMullen puffed hair off his forehead.

Andy raised a giant dark eyebrow.

They clearly weren't going to budge. Miserable heads. "Fine," I said. "We'll do yours first."

Andy waited to begin until I'd dragged in a chair. "This is going to be just a little complicated," he said as I set myself down in front of them.

The three heads glanced at each other as well as they could. Then Andy began. "First, we need you to find somebody for us."

"Just a . . . just a minute. What do you mean FIRST?"

He raised his giant brows innocently. "There are a couple of parts to the favor."

"Don't forget, you agreed!" said Lake.

"You left out the details! You did it on purpose!" I couldn't believe this.

Or maybe I could. I had no reason to believe the heads were trustworthy. It had only been a day since I'd suspected they might be flesh-eating or planet-conquering. Why was I suddenly surprised that they might be *a little tricky*?

"The favor technically has two parts," said Andy.

"*Three,*" said Lake, making a very pointed face.

"The last part is negotiable," said Andy, more to Lake than to me.

"It is non-negotiable!" said Lake.

"Baloney," muttered McMullen.

I put my head in my hands. "How many parts?" I whimpered.

"I say one," said McMullen. " 'Cause it's all going to be one giant fiasco anyway."

I had a feeling I agreed with McMullen. These guys were the worst. I took a breath and reminded myself how important this was. I needed the missing head to get my parents off the hook I had created. *That* was non-negotiable. I had to finish this. "So who do I have to find?"

"Normally I would do a drumroll here," Lake explained. "It's just: no hands."

Andy sighed. "We need you to find us a *baritone*."

"And he has to be good," Lake added.

"How's she going to know if he's any good?" McMullen said.

"A *baritone*?" I said.

"A *singer* with a *baritone range*, of course. Not the brass instrument!" Andy chuckled. Lake hooted. Even McMullen grumbled something that sounded like a laugh.

I did not think it was very funny.

"Mac has a point, we need to have auditions," Lake declared.

"Don't call me Mac! Only my son calls me Mac!" McMullen said. "And that was not my point—you're not paying attention to my points! We don't have time for auditions. We don't have time for any of this!"

"Seems like maybe you guys haven't ironed out the specifics," I said. "So maybe in the meantime you can just tell me—"

"If we're going to do this right, we're going to have auditions!" yelled Lake.

"Don't you rile him up, now," Andy said to McMullen.

"*But that's my point*, you numbskull," McMullen yelled at Lake, completely ignoring Andy. "We're not going to be able to do this right!"

"WE ARE NOT GIVING UP," Andy roared, shaking the metal table they were all on. "All for one and one for . . ."

"All!" Lake yelled enthusiastically.

"That didn't work before," McMullen grumbled.

"We'll make it work this time. Honestly, McMullen. You're almost as moody as Lake is, and you don't even have freezer burn to blame. Remember what I said, you two. The more worked up we get, the faster we defrost. We all need to be cool. Literally, please."

"You were the one yelling," McMullen said under his breath.

"That's because you're driving him nuts," Lake said under *his* breath.

"Let's all respect the defrosting schedule, folks," said Andy.

"It should take you two and a half days to defrost," I jumped in, remembering Whitney's reminder on the computer. "That's what you're on the calendar for."

"Well," Lake said smugly, "I certainly can't help it if I have a lot of brains and it takes me an extra-long time."

"I'll show you brains," said McMullen. "You just—"

"Everyone here has approximately the same amount of brains!" said Andy quickly. Then, before they could find something new to fight about, he turned his attention back to me. "So, yes, we need you to find us a baritone singer. And we'd like to hear a couple of candidates before we make our choice."

"You want me to find several baritone singers and bring them here to the lab to sing for you as part of a tryout."

"Precisely," said Andy. Then he whispered, "Although one will be just fine."

I pictured Inko Fredrickson, cremator extraordinaire, burning up my parents' hopes and dreams. "I'm on it."

Andy smiled. "Wonderful."

There was exactly one person I could think of who could sing.

I knew he could sing because I'd seen him doing it, just four months ago during the chorus section of the all-school assembly. It was hard to miss him. He'd played violin with the orchestra, then switched to play trumpet with the band, and then stood on the risers to sing. He also looked miserable, which was probably why, while the rest of my class was laughing and I was using every bit of my strength to keep clapping and not shatter into a million Igor-y pieces, I found myself staring at Howe Berger. He looked as miserable as I felt. It was uncanny.

And uncomfortably familiar.

Howe and I had avoided each other ever since second grade, when he'd performed this very serious and very elaborate puppet show for extra credit. It was called: *Who What When Where Me.* Afterwards, when I asked him a question *during the question-and-answer period*, he got this super anxious look on his face. Then, leaving the puppets all over the floor, he walked out of the room. Everybody, including our teacher, Mr. Daniels, looked at me. I didn't mean to make him walk out, but it was clear I'd done something awful, and the longer they looked, the more I started to panic, so I walked out, too. I didn't see Howe anywhere in the hall, so I just went to the girls' bathroom and hung out there worrying about everything until the vice principal came and got me. I apologized, but I didn't even know what I was apologizing for.

Okay, so there was a lot of pressure in second grade.

But also, it was pretty traumatic, him just leaving and the puppets on the ground and all those people looking at me, and I was so afraid of it happening again, of somehow the combination of us being a disaster together, that it seemed safer to avoid him. And once I was in the habit of avoiding him, the habit stuck. Plus, he got weirdly popular, or at least, popular as a weird kid, which made avoiding him even easier. I wasn't usually anywhere near the popular kids, weird or not.

On the other hand, Howe was the only kid in my grade who hadn't called me Igor in the last four months. Which, along with the fact that he could sing, made two solid reasons to call him. I was just going to have to risk the possibility that we'd end up panicking in separate bathrooms.

Those heads better be grateful.

By the time I got back to the desk, I had a plan. I looked up the phone number for the Children's Refinement Center, this place Howe's mom started about a million years ago. They had classes in all sorts of things, and everybody I knew had taken one there at some point—I, for example, had a fuzzy kindergarten-era memory of doing a terrible job in a macaroni painting class. The CRC was the only way I knew to reach Howe.

I took a deep breath and dialed.

"Thank you for calling the Children's Refinement Center of Chicago, this is Howe."

I didn't expect to get through to him so quickly, and the surprise of hearing his voice almost made me hang up. Looked like I wasn't the only one doing the Family Business thing this summer.

Before I could convince myself to speak, someone else picked up and another voice came on: "Thank you for calling the Children's Refinement Center of Chicago, this is Lanissa Berger."

"Mom," Howe said, "I have it."

"Howe?" Mrs. Berger asked over the noise of a lot of little kids yelling. "I'll take the call—can you help out by the pool?"

"Sure," he said.

"Wait!" I said, forcing myself to stop him. "I actually

want to talk to you, Howe. This is Fovea. Munson. From school."

"Oh," he said. There was a very long pause, during which we both adjusted to the fact that it was the first time we'd talked to each other on purpose in five years.

"Ooooh!" said Howe's mom.

The kids chanting in the background got clearer for a second, and I could make out what they were saying. *Throw it! In the pool!* Sounded like the refinement business was tough these days.

I cleared my throat and said, "Howe, you sing, right?"

"Ha! Is there anything he *doesn't* do?" his mom said proudly.

"This is a private conversation," Howe protested weakly.

"Okay, honey." The noise of the kids rioting got muffled, but it didn't go away—she was clearly still on the phone.

"I really don't sing," he said, almost whispering. "Is that all you wanted?"

"But you're in chorus at school. And your mom said you did. Just now."

"She was wrong."

"Howe Leonard Bernstein Berger!" Howe's mom interrupted us. Howe didn't seem that surprised. I wondered if she listened to all his calls.

"Mom," Howe said helplessly.

"Howe *loves* to sing!" his mom said.

I said, "Is there any chance you're a baritone?"

"He can fake it!" said his mom. "He's technically a tenor, but he's got very impressive range ever since his growth spurt last year."

"Mom," Howe said.

"Howe," I said, crossing all the fingers of my mind. "Would you consider singing with a couple of guys I know? Just for a little while?"

"This is a perfect professional development opportunity!" His mom sounded thrilled. "We've been waiting for something like this, and here it is, and Fovea, he'd love to do it."

He paused. "Can I speak to Fovea privately?"

"Sure!" she said.

"I mean without you on the phone?"

"Of course!" she said.

It got away! Catch it! hollered a kid in the background.

It was pretty obvious she wasn't going anywhere. I thought I heard Howe sigh, and then he asked, "Will I have to sing in front of an audience?"

"No," I assured him. That was the one thing I could guarantee.

"You promise?"

"Completely. You'd be singing with three guys. Nobody

else will be around." I didn't know if it would make a difference, but based on our history, I added, "I won't even be in there. Please?"

"He'll do it!" Howe's mom said.

"I guess I'll do it."

"How soon can you get downtown?"

After we hung up, I stared at the phone for a minute. That was easier than I thought it'd be. He was reluctant, maybe, but that seemed reasonable. I wouldn't want to help me either.

With Howe on the way, I went in search of a blindfold. It would have to be really good so he could wear it for the whole time and not have it slip. I poked around in my parents' office and found some goggles, still in their packaging. They were the extra-durable type—probably to keep gross things from squirting in your eyes while you were operating on something. Perfect. My parents wouldn't notice if a pair of goggles went missing. I found a marker and colored all over them until you couldn't see anything through the plastic. When I was done, it smelled like marker, but aside from that, it was a killer blindfold. No way would it slip.

Then I sat in the lobby, the goggles on the desk in front of me. I was ready for Howe to show up now, or as ready as I could be.

I stared out through the glass windows. Nothing.

A train rumbled by outside, but otherwise, it was quiet.

I glanced down on the desk and noticed the folder my dad had given me—I might as well do that, since I was waiting anyway. I opened it and started working through the small stack. It was mostly bills for the lab, each one with a sticky note indicating what I needed to know to pay online. After I typed in the account and password, the companies just wanted me to click the PAY button. All the rest of the info was already stored. Easy. I didn't mind paying the bill for the freezer repair or putting in the order for the extra scrubs. No, it was all going fine enough until I got to the last paper in the folder. I typed in the website at the top of the browser and the page that opened up was called Give Me a Hand, Et Cetera, LLC. I scrolled down.

No way.

That nightmare of a school assembly was coming true.

Give Me a Hand, Et Cetera, LLC, *actually sold hands, et cetera.*

Unbelievable. And frankly, considering that my parents weren't doing such a great job keeping track of the body parts they already had, I wasn't sure they should be ordering more.

I glanced back at the paper in the folder, which told me to buy one item of product number 735 for six hundred dollars.

Product number 735. I scrolled down. A leg.

A. Leg.

I was never going to unremember this.

I gritted my teeth and placed the order. Fast. And when I'd finished, I stewed and swiveled and wondered if there was any possible chance I had a secret aunt in Aruba who needed someone to sweep lizards off her porch this summer. There had to be *something* to get me away from this land of body parts, both the talking and silent varieties. Although technically, I was only assuming the leg wasn't going to talk. What did I know about anything anymore.

I'd barely leaned back in the chair when the phone rang. *Unknown*, said the caller ID.

I picked up the phone.

"Hello?" I said.

"Hello?" said a voice I sort of recognized.

"Hello?" I said again.

"Who is this?"

"Did you forget who you called?"

"No, I know who I called. But who are *you*?"

"Fovea Munson—"

"Fovea!" shrieked the other person. "Fovea! Great! It's me, Whitney!"

I nearly dropped the phone. "Whitney? What the heck! Whitney, you have to come back, this creepy guy came by, and the guys, they need you, too—"

"The guys?"

"Andy. Um. And Lake and McMullen."

"Oh! You met them! That's great, Fo, that's terrific." She lowered her voice. "They could really use more friends. That much time in the freezer, they get on each other's nerves sometimes. Ooh, I bet they're loving being defrosted, aren't they? That was all they could talk about before, and I mean, they weren't even having the easiest time talking because of being frozen—"

She faded out a little and I could hear her talking to somebody on her end. I was afraid of her hanging up, so I tried to get her attention again, saying, "Whitney, you have to come *back*—"

"Fovea, I'm sort of in a rush here, I'm in the middle of nowhere on like the last pay phone in the whole country, I think, and I don't have a lot of quarters—you can tell me what you're up to later, okay? I just, look, I think I left my phone there, in a drawer maybe, or in the conference room—"

"Yeah, I found it, and there's messages on it from—"

"Can you send it to me?"

"But—"

"I'm going to email you the address of the motel, okay, and I'll pay you back later, I promise. And also, I need you to apologize to Andy for me, okay?"

"*Okay*, but—"

And then she was gone. I sat there with the phone in

my hand. She'd tornadoed me. She hadn't listened to a word I'd said. By the time I figured out how to make that stupid complex phone dial her back, she wasn't there anymore. The phone just rang and rang and rang.

Dang.

But I could tell the heads about the call, and I'd tell them about Howe and maybe they'd soften up a little and go on and tell me where the missing specimen was. I ran back down the Hall of Innards and through the door to the lab, where I stopped short.

Not because of anything the heads were doing. I stopped because of what they weren't doing. They weren't arguing. Or laughing. They weren't doing anything. The heads were just still. Their eyes were closed. They looked like they might be—

"HEY!" I yelled. "I GOT YOU A BARITONE! *HEY!*"

"I'm awake!" Lake screamed, somehow yanking himself over so he smacked down onto the side of his head. Of his . . . him.

"Yelling is no way to wake a body up," Andy said groggily.

"You can disregard the part about the body." McMullen growled.

"AHHH!" Lake yelled from his new sideways position. "Get me up! Get me up!"

"What was that?" I said, still angry. "It wasn't funny!"

"AHHH!" Lake continued.

"We were napping," Andy said. "Napping's not supposed to be funny. It's what old fogeys like us do."

"AHHH!"

"You should really help him up," suggested Andy.

"I should *what*?"

"Because of when he was unfrozen and refrozen sideways, you know? Along with all the extra feelings, he developed a bad case of vertigo. Now he's dizzy if he isn't straight up and down. You knocked him over with all your yelling, you should help him up."

"He knocked *himself* over. He can get *himself* back up." I squatted down to Lake's eye level and turned sideways to match him. "I believe in you! You have this! Just focus!"

"AHHH!"

It did kinda pull on me to see him lying there on the cold metal table. On the other hand, I did not want to touch him. I did not. I was not. Not with a billion foot pole.

"AHHH! SO! DIZZY!"

Crud.

Well, I couldn't leave him there.

I closed my eyes and wished for a billion foot pole.

There were boxes and boxes of gloves lining the walls of the lab. Small through extra-large. *Latex* gloves, every single one of them. Great.

Since I definitely couldn't use the gloves unless I wanted to have a massive allergy attack, I was going to need something less obvious. There was nothing in either of my parents' offices that I could imagine using as a head scooper-upper. I couldn't just shovel a magazine under him like he was a bug or something—he'd be too heavy, for sure. There was the dustpan from earlier, but I wasn't convinced that would help. What if I just scooped him up and then he flipped right on over to his other side? I could get stuck doing that all day. I needed something grabby. Like tongs.

Tongs.

I ran down the hall into the conference room, flipped on the lights, and checked the trash can for yesterday's barbecue leftovers. Ace.

Salad tongs.

So. Coleslaw: apparently good for something after all.

I pulled the tongs out of the trash and ran back to the lab, where Lake was still yelling. Figuring out the best angle for grabbing was tricky since one side of his head was flat against the table. I couldn't really get much of a grip side to side; I'd have to do it front and back. "Sorry," I said as I placed one gripper at the back of his head and one in the middle of his forehead. He shut his eyes tight and in a high, unsteady voice said, "Smells like mayo?"

"Just your imagination." I squeezed the tongs. They sank into Lake's head a little bit—a side effect of defrosting,

probably. He was heavier than coleslaw, and I didn't want to pinch too hard, but amazingly, the plastic tongs were doing the job and he was actually starting to get closer and closer to upright. I'd almost gotten him there when a couple of things happened.

First the tongs slipped. Just a little.

Then a little more.

Then the doorbell buzzed.

"The doorbell!" said Andy.

"It could be a baritone," McMullen said. "Could be."

"No doubt!" Andy exclaimed. "Are you going to get that, Fovea?"

That was all fine and well, EXCEPT that *I'D* been laser-focused on the tong situation, and when the doorbell buzzed, I jumped about a foot, and the tongs slipped one more horrible time, leaving a streak of crusty mayo on Lake's forehead as he glided right out of my grasp, tilted in slow motion back down toward the table, and I, without thinking, shot my other hand out and pushed him upright. With my actual fingers.

For a second, we both stared at my hand. I did not want that hand back. Touching him was like grabbing a balloon full of frozen custard. Gross. To the absolute max.

Lake was beaming with joy. Beaming, right out from his gross frozen custard head.

"Fovea?" Andy sang. "Did you know the doorbell rang?"

I stalked out, promising myself I would never do anything with that hand again.

Nothing. Ever.

10.

HIPPOCRATES DID NOT WORRY ABOUT GETTING HIS LATIN WRONG.

OR HIS ANCIENT GREEK, FOR THAT MATTER.

I burst into the lobby, my contaminated hand safely away from me, and there was Howe Berger, standing on the other side of the glass, his hand absently checking his Afro. That was his nervous thing. I knew it from basically every time any teacher ever gave us a test. But anyway, his hair looked fine—that wasn't what made me stare.

It was the tuxedo that made me stare.

I mean, the outfit was obviously circa *before* Howe's most recent growth spurt, so it was a little tight in areas and a little short in other areas—but it was still a tux, and he still looked like a thirteen-year-old James Bond. I had a bad feeling that this situation was going to be a real letdown for Howe Berger.

I unlocked and opened the door with my usable hand. "Hi, Howe."

"Fovea." He nodded.

"Thanks for coming so quickly," I said. It had been strange talking to him on the phone, but it was even weirder talking to him face-to-face. It was clear that neither of us was used to it. I tried to stay as professional as possible and at least not *sound* nervous. "Welcome. Can I get you some water?"

He pulled at his bow tie, which seemed a little too tight, and looked around at the lobby. "What is this place?"

Did he already know? I couldn't tell. "My parents' office. They're ... doctors."

"Who's that guy?" he asked, looking at the painting.

"Hippocrates, Father of Modern Medicine. It's an unauthorized portrait," I said.

"Huh. When should I tell my mom we'll be done?" There was a bright orange minivan outside, which I assumed belonged to Howe's mom, mostly because it said THE CHILDREN'S REFINEMENT CENTER™ (RESULTS NOT GUARANTEED) across the side. It was parked directly in front of a fire hydrant. Howe's mom, an even taller, lady version of him with even more impressive hair, leaned across to the passenger-side window and gave us an epic thumbs up.

"Can you just call her when it's over?"

He frowned. "I'll see."

I held the door open while he went to find out. He leaned into the van briefly, then returned. "I can stay for an hour," he said, walking past me into the lobby and sitting down on one of the chairs. "Then my mom has errands to do."

"She can't go do them now?" I asked as I locked the door again. I didn't want her coming in and discovering her son singing with a handful of heads. I wanted her as far away as possible.

We both looked out at the orange van, so unreasonably bright in the sun that it seemed possible it was actually radioactive. After a second, Howe said, "I don't think that's going to happen."

I had no idea what the heads were planning, but it couldn't take too long. They already knew my parents would be coming back to the lab soon. And now, with Howe's mom hovering outside, there was even more reason to hurry it up, whatever *it* was. "Let's get this over with," I said.

"Do you, um, have a contract for me?" He glanced out the window.

"A what?"

"A contract?" he said again. "A written one, if possible. My mom says a verbal contract is unreliable."

"This isn't really a contract kind of situation," I said, not having any idea what a contract situation was.

He just scratched a little at his cucumber-colored cummerbund. "What kind of situation is it, then?"

"More like a charity sort of thing."

He looked unsure. "Who would I be helping?"

"A desperate girl trying to keep her parents from going to jail."

"Jail?" He edged toward the door. "That sounds kind of serious? I think you have the wrong guy."

"I didn't mean *jail* jail. I meant, like, singing jail." I tried to laugh. I was not very believable.

"That doesn't make sense."

Accurate. "I know. It doesn't make any sense at all, and it won't make sense, but honestly, I need your help. I mean the girl. Needs your help."

He picked at the sleeve of his tux like he was thinking it over.

"She's desperate." I could see him trying to find anything to hold on to.

"What about the guys I'm singing with? What's their deal?"

"They are . . . shut-ins."

"They're shut in *here*?" He looked around suspiciously. "In a doctor's office?"

"Hypochondria. And acrophobia. It's very sad."

"Uh-huh. I get that they think they're sick, but what does a fear of heights have to do with it?"

"Not heights. The one where you're afraid of crowds."

"Agoraphobia."

"You sure? That sounds like somebody who's afraid of those hairy sweaters."

"That would probably be *an*goraphobia."

"You really know your fears of things," I said, impressed.

"The Refinement Center has Latin on Thursdays," he said.

"You're still taking classes there?"

He shrugged. "It's free for me, so that's what I do summers. All summers. Forever."

"I get it," I said. "I mean, I'm here, being a receptionist."

Maybe this was going to work after all.

We both nodded silently for a minute, and I was pretty sure we were thinking the same thing. About how summer break was basically a sham. About how easy it was to get stuck someplace, like a book in the wrong library section that nobody would ever actually read. About—

"Is that a betta fish or a guppy?" Howe asked.

I reminded myself that this was business, not friend-making time. "So will you do the singing thing?"

He glanced toward the front door.

"If you're going to be here for an hour anyway, it couldn't hurt anything, right?"

He looked back to me. "I guess not. Except—"

"What?"

"Why are *you* organizing it?"

Howe was easier to talk to than I'd thought he'd be, but that didn't mean I trusted him with any part of the truth. "There's a chance I might know the desperate girl."

His eyes narrowed on me for a second.

"Betta fish, by the way," I said. "Not guppy."

We both looked at the tank, which was easier than looking at each other. Then he nodded. "Okay. I guess I'll take a verbal contract. I, Howe Berger, will sing with some shut-ins for about an hour for charitable purposes."

Then he stood and shook my hand.

Oh, let me recap.

He finally agreed to do it, and everything was going well. And then.

HE SHOOK MY HAND.

Technically, I guess I'd been holding it out, so it might have looked like an invitation. But now WE BOTH HAD DISGUSTING FROZEN CUSTARD HEAD ALL OVER OUR HANDS. *It was spreading*—for just a second, I wondered if this was how the zombie plague was going to happen. I tried to stop myself from hyperventilating. I closed my eyes and imagined myself glopping around in a sea of hand sanitizer. In my imagination, I directed a giant hand to pick Howe up and drop him into the sea, too, tuxedo and all. We glopped together. Plague averted.

"Stay here," I said, opening my eyes and feeling much calmer. This picturing strategy was working. "And *don't touch anything.*" I left and came back seconds later with a huge bottle of lavender-scented hand sanitizer that I pillaged from my mom's desk. "You want this," I told Howe as he looked at me suspiciously. "Trust me." I squirted large amounts of goo all over our hands and then I explained the plan while we squeegeed the stuff around until it dried.

"So," he said when I was done, "I have to be blindfolded because of the agoraphobia?"

"It's pretty bad."

He seemed to consider it for a minute. "Okay. I'll be

blindfolded. But for future reference, I'm guessing this is the kind of thing that goes in the contract."

"Andy, Lake, McMullen, this is Howe."

"This is how what?" Lake asked.

"No, this is Howe," I said. "That's his name. He's your baritone."

"Am I facing them?" Howe whispered.

"Yes," I said.

"Baloney," McMullen grumbled. "He's awfully young-looking."

"We're awfully old-looking," Lake sang. "And does anybody smell lavender?"

I pretended not to hear the last bit, and hoped they weren't going to be too picky about Howe. For the sake of my school reputation, I needed this to go smoothly. Also, it wasn't like I had a ton of baritones up my sleeve. "He can sing baritone, isn't that what matters?"

"That is exactly what matters," Andy said. "Young man, let's do a little singing, shall we?"

"I'm ready whenever you are," Howe said, standing straight again.

"Now, have you ever been in a barbershop quartet?"

"No."

They started talking music, and then the doorbell rang,

making me jump a foot. "I'm going to get that," I said, but they were so involved in four-part harmony this and tenor that and bass whatever that I just slipped right out and they didn't even notice.

"How come the box is in a bag?" I asked the deliveryman out front. It wasn't the same guy from before, but definitely the same company—I wondered briefly how many people were running around Chicago wearing berets and carrying boxes of body parts. Probably safe to say too many. This particular guy had a smallish box that he was holding in a clear bag.

"Oh yeah. Started leaking. Have a nice day."

Nice. As if. In my opinion, no day that involved a body part in a baggie should ever be considered *nice.* I walked back down the Hall of Innards toward the lab, holding the small biohazard out in front of me. This day had been all kinds of things, but nice definitely wasn't one of them. And shoot. It wasn't even lunchtime.

I stepped into the lab.

"Well, no use having an unconscious baritone," McMullen grumbled.

Howe was passed out on the floor, the blindfold lying next to him.

What.

"I was gone for a single minute!" I shouted, not sure

whether I should keep holding the bag or put it down and help Howe. "Who took off his blindfold?!"

The guys looked at me innocently, all big eyes and eyebrows up. Well, Andy and Lake did. McMullen looked as cheesed off as I felt.

"We didn't touch a thing," Lake said. "No hands."

"You know that is not what I mean! I mean, who *said he could take off the blindfold*? What am I going to do with him now?"

"Slap him!" Lake crowed.

"Cold water," Andy advised.

"That's not WHAT I MEAN!" I took a couple of breaths. I walked over to the body parts freezer. I opened it very quickly, shoved the bag in, and slammed the door behind me before anything else could get out and drive me crazy. It felt good to slam something. "I mean, what am I going to do now that he has SEEN YOU? There's no reason for Howe to keep you a secret. He could tell everybody at school, and *this is the absolute last thing I need at school*. He could tell everybody at the Children's Refinement, *his mom*, who I am pretty sure would not exactly keep a lid on this sort of thing. I'm going to have to move to Alaska. And if he tells anybody that I let him *hang out* with you, that's going to be bad news for my parents, really, super-bad news. Maybe as bad as them losing that other head. Guy. Whatever."

And then I heard some movement from the floor.

"It's okay," Howe said, sounding a little woozy. "I really want to work on the album."

I turned to the heads. "The what?"

Andy smiled somewhat toothlessly.

I did not smile back.

11.

HIPPOCRATES DID NOT GET TANGLED UP IN TIGER KIDNAPPINGS

"Four-part harmonies, a lot of 1920s music, maybe a little experimentation," Andy was saying. I couldn't see him because my head was in my hands and my eyes were closed. This was spiraling out of control was what it was doing.

"Stop," I said. "Stop everything. Nothing else is happening until you tell me the whole favor. Every single part." Howe looked up from the floor where he sat, holding the emergency ice pack I'd found.

"You got us a baritone," Andy said. "Next is the recording session."

"And then the wrap party," said Lake. "*Non*-negotiable."

I was starting to get a headache. "How..."

"Yes?" said Howe.

"Not you," I said weakly. "How... is all this going to happen?"

"We'd been planning this for a while, and we were counting on Whitney, but then she left..."

McMullen added, "Plus the whole—"

"Never mind that," Andy jumped in, cutting him off. "Now we have you and we have Howe, who will do splendidly, by the way, and thank you." Howe beamed. "The next step will be the little recording session."

"I don't know how to do that kind of thing," I said.

"I see," said Andy. "Well, that's fair. You being new to the music business and all. It shouldn't be that hard. You just call up some places, see who has availability to come out and record a quick session here. Tonight, that is. It should really be tonight."

"Tonight."

"The later in the evening, the better. That will certainly help guarantee that your parents don't discover us in the middle of the Delaware, so to speak."

McMullen grunted. "Middle of the—just talk like normal people, Andy."

"And then a party?" I asked. "I don't throw parties."

"Never?" Lake asked incredulously.

I shook my head.

"Not New Year's?" he asked. "Solstice? Día de los Muertos? Not even *birthday parties*?"

I shook my head again. "You never know if anybody's going to show up. It's too risky."

"I agree," said Howe. "Parties: risky."

Huh. It was nice having somebody agree with you. That hadn't happened to me in months.

"Well, this will be a crash course for both of you!" Lake said. "I'll teach you. You can be my protégés. This will be marvelous."

I took the bag of ice away from Howe and put it right between my eyes. "How many people need to be at this party?"

"As many as possible," said Lake.

"And *then* you tell me where the you-know-what is?"

"Then we tell you where the you-know-*who* is."

"The you-know-who-what?" Howe asked. "Is there more I should know about this?"

Oh, what the heck—he'd already seen the worst of it. If he was going to flambé what was left of my reputation, he had more than enough information already. I sighed. "There's a missing head. The ex-boyfriend of the former lab receptionist is using the missing head as romantic blackmail. But she's in Florida, somewhere, and didn't get the message, besides which, she should probably not be giving this guy any more chances because he's a creepazoid *and* a cremator."

"Double whammy," murmured Howe.

I nodded. "I don't want my parents to get in trouble, so I'm finding the head before he reports it missing and they get shut down or go to jail or whatever the penalty is for losing a head."

"It can't be good, that's for sure."

I pushed the ice harder into my face. It was the perfect kind of unbearable. "But these guys won't tell me where the other head is until I do their massively unending favor."

"It's like a blackmail and a counterblackmail," Howe said. "Or extortion."

"Gentle coercion, really," said Andy.

"I did a report once on a book called *Heists and Other Schemes*. This almost qualifies as a Tiger Kidnapping," said Howe. "*If* you were also going to make the missing head open a bank vault. Wait. Or maybe Fovea opens the bank vault belonging to the missing head?"

"Ooh, tell me more about a Tiger Kidnapping!" Lake said. "I like the sound of that one."

"You would," said McMullen.

They continued discussing the technical terms of how exactly they were ruining my life while ice water dribbled slowly down my nose. I halfheartedly swiped at the dribble. Being ganged up on by three heads and Howe Berger was not making me feel very good about myself.

Eventually, I reminded the guys that we were on a limited timetable and I left them to practice while I found somebody to come record the album. Out in the lobby, I looked up recording studios. I could hear the guys down the hall taking Howe through what they were going to sing on the album. They sounded pretty sharp. It absolutely did not make up for what they were putting me through, but at least the music was decent.

I dialed the number for AHHH Recording Studios. Maybe this crazy plan was possible.

"Our first available appointments are at the beginning of October."

Or maybe not. "Your first appointment is in *four months*?"

"Do you want it?"

"No, thanks."

The second place I called was even more depressing.

"First of all, I've never heard of you," said the snippy man who answered the phone. "We don't do walk-ins. And secondly, no one, *no one* in this business is going to go to where *you* are. My advice? Buy yourself a cheap microphone and spend a few years working up your game."

I hung up. He didn't know anything about my game.

Plus, *years*? Please. I had less than twenty-four hours before Inko ratted on my parents and they paid the price. A new and terrible thought washed over me, giving me straight-up goose bumps. If that head was still alive, or whatever Lake and Andy and McMullen were, and my parents didn't take care of it properly, could they be charged with *murder*? They couldn't be charged with murder, could they? And how long did it take for somebody who was already dead to die?

My mouth went dry. Worst-case scenario here was becoming really, really bad.

As I clicked on link after link, and called one disagreeable recording studio after another, I tried to fight the feeling that the favor was doomed, that this was as far as I was going to get. Soon I ran out of recording studios, and was just calling anywhere in the area that mentioned music. I almost let myself get talked into guitar lessons by somebody at a music school, but aside from that, I wasn't getting anywhere until I clicked on the link for a place called Nussbaum's Musicalarium.

The link took me to a single sad page that looked like it had been made when the internet was first invented. In the middle of the page was a roughly drawn bird whose beak blinked open and shut. When it was open, a music note appeared above the bird.

I picked up the phone, and after a few rings, a woman answered.

We worked out the details. Like the snippy guy predicted, they didn't make house calls. But after a few minutes, I'd booked us a recording session.

It looked like we were going to visit Nussbaum's Musicalarium.

I stepped back into the lab, and they broke off in the middle of a song. "We've got a recording session scheduled," I announced, and they cheered.

"My hour's almost up." Howe straightened his bow tie. "Just so you know."

"Short rehearsal," grumbled McMullen. "We barely got one run-through."

"It'll come together," encouraged Lake.

"Who's coming to do the recording?" Andy asked.

I shifted a little. "Somebody named Nussbaum. We'll, um, be going to Nussbaum's Musicalarium." They all started talking at once.

"Wait—"

"Going?"

"We're *going*?"

"We're GOING SOMEPLACE!" cried Lake. "What'll I *WEAR*! Kidding, kidding, but oh, this is great news."

"Are you sure about this?" Andy asked.

I shook my head. "It was the only way I could get anybody to agree to do it. But no, thanks for asking, I'm not sure about it. We need to figure out how to keep everybody from seeing you and obviously blindfolds aren't going to work—"

"Sorry," Howe said.

"—but at least it's only about fifteen blocks away from here. So it could be worse."

"When?" Howe asked.

"Tonight. The only time they had in the next twenty-four hours was midnight."

"The stroke of midnight!" said Lake. "An inspiring time for creativity! The Chunnel between dead of night and dead of morning!"

"Get a grip," said McMullen.

"Fovea?" Howe sort of half raised his hand, the too-small tuxedo jacket keeping him from raising it all the way. "I need to go."

"I'll walk you out," I said, and we stepped into the Hall of Innards. About halfway down, I slowed. I wanted to thank him, but it suddenly felt weird. "Is your head okay from when you landed on it?"

He nodded, then stopped. "Except I probably shouldn't nod for a little while."

"I didn't know it was going to be this complicated. When I called you."

"But you did know they were heads," he said.

"Well, yeah."

"That's just . . ."

"I know."

"The weirdest."

"I know."

"Are we going to cover this in eighth-grade biology, do you think?"

"I asked them. They kind of dodged it. Anyway, sorry to get you involved. I just thought that blindfold thing would work. I didn't count on them being so sneaky. They're really sneaky for not having bodies."

"It could happen to anyone."

"Thanks."

He nodded. "Ow."

"And thanks for not telling anyone about any of this," I said.

"The truth is, my mom's birthday is next month." He reached up to fidget with his hair. "I, um, needed to get her something. An album of music I recorded secretly will be perfect. So it's really no problem." He stopped. "Actually, there *is* a problem. I'm not really that experienced in the sneaking-around department."

"Oh." I wasn't exactly an expert either. "Well, sneaking shouldn't be that complicated, right? Let's meet here. Then we can grab the guys and all go together to the recording place. The heads aren't walking there on their own, plus it'll be safer to sneak as a group."

"What about before all that? How do we get *here*?"

I could probably get as far as the Holography Museum with my eyes closed, I knew it so well—that was about halfway. I'd never made the trip to the lab in the middle of the night, but there were streetlights. If I ran, it would only take a couple of minutes. "I'm going to walk. Or run. Probably run-walk. I live close by."

"*I* don't. It would take me almost an hour from my house."

"I guess you could take the train?"

He recoiled, gasping, like somebody had told him he could never wear a tuxedo again. "The train is dangerous at night. And often in the daytime."

"Don't they have judo classes or something at the CR?"

"Only tai chi."

"So just defend yourself."

"Tai chi is about the movement of energy. It's not about beating people up."

"You can't move your energy into fighting someone?"

"I don't think that's part of the rules."

"Then I don't know." I realized it wasn't something I

was looking forward to either. Running around at night. On the scale of one to dangerous, it was straight-up dangerous. Howe picked the lint out of his cummerbund, looking slightly less James Bond–y. As he flicked the fuzz away, he leaned back against one of my dad's drawings of a spleen mid-surgery and knocked it off the wall. He caught the drawing before it fell far, but ripped one armpit of the jacket.

"Dag," he said, examining the tear. "Now my tux looks weird."

NOW it looks weird? I wanted to say, but then I had a brilliant idea. "That's it. We make ourselves look weird. For the sneaking out. People leave you alone if you look weird."

He still looked unsure. "You never know where danger lurks."

"Tell me about it." I nodded toward the lab. "But, okay? Does that work? It's the only idea I've got."

"Okay. We'll meet here, make the record, and have a party?"

"The party," I said, "is something I haven't totally figured out."

He shrugged. "I don't go to many parties myself."

"Maybe I'll bring streamers? That'll be fine, right?"

"Sure," Howe said. "I'll see if I can think of anything to bring."

Before I could say anything, we heard a soft click: the unmistakable sound of the blue door at the end of the hall gently closing. We glanced at each other, identical looks of alarm across our faces, and then ran toward the lobby.

She was right in the middle of it, the clean chicken adobo dish in her lap.

Grandma Van.

"Oh, hello," she said.

I had no idea how long she'd been there, but she had keys. She could have let herself in at any point. And the scuff marks on the walls indicated she'd had enough time to change directions more than once. We stared at each other for a moment and then Grandma Van said, "Well, here's your dish." Except that she said it very carefully, like there was some kind of secret message, and then she gave us both a long, meaningful look and drove her chair out. The dish was still on her lap. We watched as she drove down the sidewalk, the scooter bumping slightly over the cracks in the cement. She motored past Howe's parallel-parked mom, played chicken with a couple pushing a stroller, and then drove out of view. Howe looked at me.

I felt like apologizing, but I wasn't sure what for. "That was my grandma."

"Oh. Does she have memory problems?"

"I don't think so. I think she just likes to mess with people."

"Huh."

"Yeah."

And then, with nothing else for us to discuss, Howe left, exactly one hour after he'd arrived, precisely as the verbal contract had stated. I hoped I wasn't making a gigantic mistake by trusting him. But it was too late to back out.

It was for real now.

12.

HIPPOCRATES DID NOT HAVE TO SNEAK OUT OF HIS OWN HOUSE

On the walk home at the end of the day, something finally broke awesome.

My mom got a call. The ringtone was my grandmother's—a song called "Old Lady & the Devil." I wasn't paying much attention because I was obsessively replaying every conversation with Howe, sure I'd screwed something up somewhere. But then my mom hung up and stopped us in the middle of the sidewalk, a giant smile on her face. "Guess who decided to eat in the Swan Song's dining hall tonight?"

"Seriously?" I couldn't believe it.

"Did she fall out of the scooter and hit her head?" asked my dad.

"Nope," my mom said happily. "I think for the first time ever, she decided to take my advice and try something new!"

We passed the museum, and I smiled in the general direction of the banana.

Then we ordered pizza when we got home, to celebrate.

I have to admit, at the time, I really thought that phone call from Grandma Van was a sign that things were going to go smoothly.

Five hours later, I was lying in bed, in the dark, dressed as a left kidney.

It was exactly 10:45 p.m.

I had an hour and fifteen minutes to meet Howe at the lab, pack the heads, and get to the recording studio. It was going to be close, but I'd needed to wait until my parents were definitely asleep.

Sneaking out was one of those things I never actually thought I'd try, like getting a beehive hairdo or eating live roaches. I felt like a completely different person.

I rolled out of bed quietly, spylike, and the bottom part

of the too-big kidney costume slumped against my knees. It had been my dad's Halloween costume from the year before—he and my mom went as a pair of kidneys. Hers was smaller and definitely would have fit better, but I was going to need the bigger, baggier one to make my escape.

There had been a lot to plan out.

I'd decided against the classic fake body situation. My parents would have immediately noticed that it wasn't anatomically correct, even under the covers, and that would have bothered them even more than me having left a fake body in the first place. "How could *our daughter* think that a hip joint bent like this?" I could hear the total wilt of disappointment.

I did leave a note, though. I went with *BRB*. It seemed casual enough that maybe they wouldn't freak out if they discovered me gone in the middle of the night. Also, it was a teeny bit comforting to me. Like maybe I actually would BRB.

Then I slung my backpack on over the kidney costume and snuck through the dark apartment. I was picturing myself as a stealthy night cat, but a lumpy section of the kidney bumped a side table, and there was a loud clang as my mom's bronzed gallstone fell over.

Removing that gallstone was my mom's first-ever surgery, and she'd wanted the occasion memorialized.

Personally, I'd always avoided touching the gallstone—even though it was covered in bronze, it had been *in somebody's gallbladder*. I thought that was enough reason to not put it in the front hall, but, as usual, the vote was two against one. So I wasn't surprised when it ratted me out, clanking onto its side and then rocking back and forth, like it was laughing at me. I froze, ready to scram back to my room if I heard any sound from my parents.

Nothing.

I unfroze, fixed the gallstone, and kept moving forward.

The front door was now a few steps away. My dad's keys were in the key dish, which was actually a mangled pottery-camp drink coaster. The keys were always there, but it hadn't kept me from checking obsessively all evening. I lifted them slowly so they didn't clink against the coaster, then eased open the front door and ducked out into the hallway. I hit the down button for the elevator and waited, hoping none of my neighbors were around. The costume included a hood and I pulled it over my head, even though probably anyone in the building would instantly know that the short, shifty kidney was me. When the elevator arrived, I got on, feeling my guts dip as it started to drop to the lobby.

The floor numbers counted down silently and I tugged the hood lower. With a gentle bump, the elevator landed on the ground floor. I stepped out and immediately ducked around the corner, hiding behind the huge planter with the fake palm tree.

This was the trickiest part. Past the elevators in the opposite direction was a small office, and in that office, there was a night watchman. I'd been in there. I'd seen how the security camera pointed toward the front door and played endlessly on the little black-and-white screen, I knew there was no way I could avoid it. But every time I'd been in there, I'd noticed something else, too. That wasn't the only screen. There was another one, and it was bigger, and it was full color, and it always had a game on it. Football, basketball, whatever was in season. I had to gamble that it was on again tonight. And that it was more interesting than the little black-and-white screen. And that as long as I didn't make any quick moves, the night watchman wasn't going to be distracted.

I glommed along the wall as far as I could until I knew I was almost in range of the camera. Then I squatted down a little, letting the kidney costume come to rest just above my ankles. I was trying my best to resemble nothing more than an unimpressive blob, just a technical problem with the screen. I took a breath and, still in a squat, slowly edged out. I scooted, then stopped. Scooted, then stopped. No fast movements. If the watchman on duty glanced at the screen, I wanted to look like Nothing. The kind of Nothing that you know has been there the whole time, you just never noticed it before. The kind of Nothing you don't ask questions about or expect things of.

Inch by inch, I made my way to the door. I got about halfway there before I started to feel like the plan was actually working.

The other thing that happened about halfway there: I realized why people do squats for exercise.

Holy kidney.

I didn't know how I was going to stand when I finally made it to safety.

When I got to the door, I slipped out in one slow, smooth, non-attention-grabbing move. A bead of sweat was rolling down my face, partly from the costume and partly from the squatting, but I couldn't relax until I was completely out of range. When I finally made it, I tipped over onto the sidewalk, stretching my legs to the sky and making a mental note that I didn't think I was going to be able to get back in the same way.

I used the wall to pull myself up on my jelly legs, and then looked around.

I'd made it.

I'd snuck out. I was loose on the streets of nighttime Chicago.

Every part of me was more awake than ever before. And *the night* was somehow awake, too. All my edges felt clear and sharp, like I was made of lasers. I pushed back the hood of the kidney costume and let it hang down, just feeling the air around my head. The air outside my building was the most amazing air I'd ever breathed. It was sweet and it was clean and it was electric and for the first time, I actually believed I could pull the whole thing off.

I started to run. Running made me even more sure I could pull it off. Running does not usually give me positive feelings, but right then, in the middle of the night, it was incredible. It was exhilarating, like being shot from a slingshot. Like having a destiny. I ran down the sidewalk away from our building, my backpack slapping at me over the costume. I aimed for the pools of streetlight so that any lurking dangers would be able to see that I was a kidney and just leave me alone.

When I arrived at 11:05 p.m., out of breath and pushing at a cramp in my ribs, Howe was already waiting out front, still in his tux, but now looking additionally weird with vegetables on strings all around his neck and sporting a small turquoise fanny pack.

And next to him, leaning against the wall with her arms crossed, was Em Taylor.

13.

HIPPOCRATES DID NOT GET AMBUSHED

Oh heck, no, I thought.

14.

HIPPOCRATES
DID NOT GET THE
PANIC SWEATS

"Hey, Eyeballs," she said. "Why are you wearing the kidney?"

I glared meaningfully at Howe.

He looked back at me, completely *un*meaningfully.

"Howe," I said, as calmly as I could. "I need to talk to you inside. Alone."

15.

HIPPOCRATES DID NOT GET EATEN BY A (METAPHORICAL) OWL

So, by the way.

The assembly at school?

That wasn't actually the spectacular moment that ended my friendship with Em.

That moment was after the assembly.

What with the amount of slouching and sweating I'd done during the concert, my T-shirt and jeans stuck to me in weird places as we filed back to our homerooms. All the other classes looked half-asleep. *My* class was having the time of their lives slumping down the hall with limps and hunchbacks, miming their sacks of knuckles or whatever, and doing it to the everlasting mystification of Ms. Peters, who had somehow missed the entire thing.

I stood in the middle of the line, staring ahead of me at Igor impression after Igor impression, every single one making me feel worse than the one before it. I could hear them behind me, too. It wasn't just that they were trying to make me feel bad. It was how much fun they were having doing it.

I could actually feel myself disappearing into the joke.

Our line moved onward, slowly creeping forward in the hallway traffic jam, and the next time we passed a bathroom, I slipped inside. Empty. I closed my eyes and tried to breathe again. I'd need to come up with an excuse for why I was late when I eventually got back to class, but I didn't care. One more second in that line of Igors and I might have come apart, just crumbled into pieces, exactly the sort of pieces, in fact, that an Igor might have liked.

I turned on the cool water and let it run over my hands.

Maybe, I forced myself to think, it will be okay.

I could stay in the bathroom, running water over my hands until everyone else got old and died.

No. That plan was no good.

I was going to have to leave the bathroom.

Just.

Not yet.

The sound of Em laughing echoed in my head. I tried to push it down, to bury it somewhere I'd never look. In my anklebones, maybe. I never went there.

I splashed some water on my face, and then, as I reached for a paper towel, the bathroom door opened, startling me, and I dove blindly into a stall. I'd barely pulled the lock when I heard someone say, "Fovea?"

Em.

What was she doing?

Maybe she hadn't realized what I'd known all along, that having parents who experimented on dead bodies was bad for a person's reputation. Maybe she was there to apologize. Maybe. I stood in that tiny space, as still as possible. Water rolled down my nose and got the front of my shirt wet.

"Fo?" she said. Her voice echoed a little off the tiles. "Ms. Peters saw you come in here and sent me to see if you were okay."

I was not okay.

"Fovea? I know you're in here. I can see your feet right now."

Stupid gravity. Stupid feet.

"Fovea. I don't know what you're freaking out about. It's no big deal."

It's no big deal. She'd said that before, at zoo camp. *This is natural selection. Natural selection doesn't care what plans you had.*

Oh. I was the tarantula here.

This was my life cycle.

My life cycle was an embarrassment.

"Are we..." I ran out of words and had to start again. "Are we friends?"

She sighed deeply, like this was all a huge hassle. "Eh."

"Why?" I took a breath to steady my voice. To keep it matter-of-fact. "Why'd you replace me with Dana? Was it something I said?"

"No."

"We did all those things—"

"*We* didn't do them. *I* did. You were just there."

"What?"

There was a short pause, exactly long enough for an owl to scoop up a tarantula in its beak.

"You're boring."

Crunch.

"So, I'll just tell Ms. Peters you'll be out in a little while."

I'd really believed that Em would come back to me in the end, and that Dana was just a phase. I'd been wrong. The food chain of life is about the most permanent thing there is, I thought to myself. And then the door slammed behind her, and Em was gone and I'd been swallowed by something bigger than me, with no way out.

Except for being digested or barfed up, but that sort of confuses the analogy.

And this was pretty clear. Em had cut me loose.

By the time I finally left the bathroom, I knew where I stood. I was a holographic banana in full daylight. A cosmic joke, and also utterly, completely invisible.

16

HIPPOCRATES DID NOT GET TANGLED UP IN REGULAR KIDNAPPINGS EITHER

11:25 p.m.

The night of the recording.

Em was not supposed to be standing outside the lab.

I should never have trusted Howe.

I unlocked the front door, ushered Howe in, and pulled the door closed behind the two of us. Turning on the light seemed too risky. A passing cop might think there was a break-in or something. Anyway, the glow from Herophilus's tank and the streetlamp outside was enough to see by. Em was watching us through the window, and I turned my back to her so she wouldn't see my face.

Before I could say anything, though, Howe whispered, "Guess what? The train wasn't so bad after all. And on the way here, I calculated that as long as we leave by eleven thirty, we'll get there by midnight. So it's totally okay that you're late. We haven't even been waiting long."

"I am not late!" I whispered back. "Anyway, even if I was, THAT ISN'T THE POINT."

"What's the point, then?"

"Who put this together? Was it Dana? Devon?"

". . . You did, right? Or else I don't know what you're talking about."

"What is she doing here?"

"I invited her," he said, reaching into the turquoise fanny pack to pull out a schedule he'd written down. He'd already scratched off *11 p.m., travel by train to lab.* "You can keep that for reference. I have another one."

"Why would you invite her? What were you thinking?"

He looked sheepish as he zipped the fanny pack. "The guys made me promise I'd try to invite more people. For the party, you know. They can be *very persuasive.*"

"So there's no plan? But why HER?"

"Oh." He frowned. "Well, my mom and I ran into Em and her mom in the grocery store, and it sort of came up."

"Tell me exactly."

"Okay, well, there was an awkward moment in the frozen food, and it was really cold and uncomfortable, and our mothers were talking, and I just sort of said, 'Hey, saw your friend Fovea at the lab today while we were not doing anything in particular.' And *she* said, 'You went to the lab?' And then she demanded to be included in whatever it was we were doing."

"Howe—"

"Also, the guys were *very persuasive* about more people at the party. You know how tricky they are. I figured I could catch two birds with one birdcage."

"You mean kill two birds with one stone?"

"Oh, no. That sounds awful. I'm opposed to bird cruelty. Not that cages are much better, I guess. . . ."

"*Howe.* Have you even been to school in the last few months? Have you seen me and Em be friends in the last few months?"

"What—are you guys in a fight?"

"Are we in a *fight*? We are in an apocalypse, Howe. We are in an atom bomb."

"Why'd she come, then?"

"She's always wanted to come to the lab."

"*Or* maybe the fight isn't as bad as you think it is."

I glanced through the window at her. That wasn't possible.

But.

"Did she know I was going to be here?"

"Yep."

If there was even the smallest chance that he was right, I had to find out. "How much did you tell her?"

"About the guys?"

I nodded.

"Nothing. Our moms were there, so I was being very cryptic. All she knows is that we're 'doing' 'something.'"

"Well, that definitely is cryptic."

"Thanks."

The night had barely started and it was already a mess. On one hand, if we sent Em away, she'd be angry. Any chance at being friends again would be out. She might also be angry enough to tell her mom, who could tell my parents. It was risky. If word got back to my parents, Howe and I would get in serious trouble for sneaking into the lab in the middle of the night.

And if she stayed, she would see the heads. I wasn't worried about her fainting or throwing up, or even being too surprised. She'd probably think they were awesome. If anybody could handle it, she could. That wasn't a problem.

But it would cement my spot in history as an actual Igor. Even worse, if there *was* any chance that we could be friends again, I'd never be sure whether she was being my actual friend, or if she was just using me to hang out with the heads. They'd become the next Dana. I could already see it.

Em tapped on the window, making me jump. *Well?* she mouthed.

Then there was the third possibility. Maybe it would fix everything. Maybe this was my chance.

"Howe," I said slowly. "You really didn't mean to ruin my life? I mean, ruin it more?"

"No!"

"Okay, then you want to make it up to me?"

He nodded.

"Your head's feeling better?"

He nodded again.

"Great. So, do you remember what we did with those blindfold-goggles?"

11:26 p.m.

I left Em sitting on one of the uncomfortable chairs in the lobby, guarded by Howe. I didn't actually think Howe could keep her from following me, but I was counting on him at least distracting her.

"So, Howard," I heard her say.

"It's just Howe."

"So costumes, huh. Why all the vegetables?"

"It was strategic," Howe explained. "I thought that if

anything went wrong, at least we'd have something to live on. Part of a wilderness survival class I took once . . ."

I stepped into the Hall of Innards, leaving their voices behind and completely unprepared for how dark it was. It gave me the spooks. I tried to find the switch, thinking about the upside to all this, which was that at least I'd gotten a lot less boring in the last twenty-four hours. Maybe the key to Em was that. I just needed to show her that I wasn't boring. Starting with the lab. I hit the light, blinked as my eyes adjusted to the brightness, and hustled down the hall to the wet lab.

Inside, the guys were doing some vocal warm-ups. They stopped as soon as they saw me.

"Sorry to interrupt," I said. "One quick thing to take care of before we get ready to go."

"We can't be late," Lake said. "Recording studios don't like that."

"We can make up the time," I said, scanning the counters in the lab. "This is important. I need some very specific eye protection."

11:29 p.m.

I ran back into the lobby with the blindfold-goggles.

Em turned in the chair. "So when do I get to see the lab? And especially the bodies. When do I get to see the bodies?"

"That's not happening," I said. And then, when she

started to frown, I added, "Right now. That's not happening *right now.*"

"What *is* happening?" she asked. "You guys are in costumes. Hanging out in the middle of the night." She leaned toward me and lowered her voice. "Is this what you do now?"

"No. No, no, no. *This*"—I gestured around the lab—"is definitely *not* what I do. I never come here. One night only."

"And yesterday," Howe said helpfully. "You were also here yesterday."

"Howe," I whispered. "Please stop helping."

"What are we even talking about?" asked Em impatiently. "I snuck out because *he*"—she pointed fiercely at Howe—"promised me some lab adventure while I was stuck in frozen food products and bored out of my mind. So far, no adventure. No lab. Sneaking out was cool, but I can do that on my own, thanks."

I grabbed a strand of Howe's broccoli and pulled him next to me at the desk. Time for the super-totally-half-baked plan we invented while she was waiting outside.

"Em Taylor," I said as officially as I could, "as Left Kidney, I'd like to welcome you to your first outing with the Underground Chicago Adventurers'..."

Not "club." That sounded like something for little kids. Not "league" either. That sounded sporty. I looked to Howe for help.

"Refinement," he said.

It would have to do.

"Refinement," I said.

"You have a secret club? With him?"

Howe and I shared an awkward nod.

"And you've done a lot of these middle of the night adventure things?"

"Well—" said Howe.

"A few," I said, hoping he'd roll with it.

"Some," said Howe.

"Yeah," I said. "And since this is your first time at the Chicago Underground—"

"Underground *Chicago*," said Howe.

"Underground *Chicago* Adventurers' Refinement, we're going to need you to be blindfolded." I handed her the blindfold-goggles. She held them up. The key to our potential friendship dangled between us. She smelled them, wrinkling her nose, then pulled them on. After a second, she pushed them high on her forehead.

"No thanks," she said.

Howe and I looked at each other. The half-baked plan depended on her agreeing to be blindfolded. Without that, the plan wasn't baked at all.

"That doesn't make any sense," she continued. "How am I supposed to have an adventure if I'm blindfolded?

That's just weird. You guys have fun with your Kidney and Vegetables Club. I'm going home." She stood.

"Wait," I said, trying not to sound as desperate as I felt. She couldn't leave. I had to ask her. "Why did you come tonight?"

She shrugged. "So I could see the lab. Obviously. Also, Dana's in Cleveland. The last two days have been pretty boring."

Boring. That was familiar.

"Also, just so you know," she said, pulling on the goggles one more time. "These things really stink. They smell like felt tip marker, and nobody's going to want to wear them." She looked around. "That said, they black out everything pretty well. I can't see a thing."

"Howe," I said, thinking quickly. "Give me some broccoli. Now."

11:35 p.m.

Em was now completely tangled in broccoli, kale, garlic, peppers, and blue yarn. Her arms were tied down by her sides, thick with broccoli. She had a kale scarf. Her hands were useless and extremely garlicky. And the blindfold-goggles were still on.

"You misheard me, Kidney Face. I said I was *not* doing the adventure."

We were five minutes late. Maybe we could make up the time on the walk to the recording studio. That could work.

"You were bored," I said. "Now you're not."

11:36 p.m.

Howe and I left Em in the lobby and walked quickly down the Hall of Innards.

"Thanks," I said. "For loaning me your vegetables so I could tie up my ex–best friend."

"Anytime," said Howe, rearranging the couple of vegetable strands he had left. "I mean, I don't exactly think it's a good idea. But I'm also not sure any of this is technically a good idea."

"Excellent point," I said as we stepped into the lab and the heads all started talking at the same time. "Hold on, everybody. There's a slight adjustment to the plan. We're bringing somebody along with us. And this is important: she can't know about you. We have to keep her from knowing that you're—"

Lake interrupted. "Devastatingly handsome?"

"No. That you don't have bodies."

"That's going to be a tough one," he said thoughtfully. "I mean, I'm good at impressions, but—"

"No," I said. "No, no—you don't have to *do* anything. Please *don't* do anything, actually. She's wearing the

blindfold I made for Howe's tryout. And she's sort of...
tied up. So she won't be taking the blindfold off either. But
if you mention that you are just heads, even subliminally,
I'm bringing you back immediately."

"That seems fair," said Andy.

"Great. So we're all agreed? No talking about not having bodies?"

"When do we ever do that?" asked Lake.

"When do you ever *not* talk about it," grumbled
McMullen. "Ever since we got to the freezer, it's been, 'I
miss my feet,' 'I miss my knees,' 'I miss my—'"

"I believe we can accommodate you," said Andy, cutting off what was clearly about to become another yelling
match. "Gentlemen?"

They mumbled in agreement.

"Great," I said. "We have to move fast to make up time."

Andy told us where to find some coolers, and while
the heads discussed our outfits like we weren't even there,
Howe and I started digging around under the big sink.

"That one?" Howe asked, pointing at a smallish lunch-
size cooler that would probably hold one head comfortably.
I nodded, slid it out, and handed it to him. He opened it and
checked inside. Empty, thankfully. "So why did you guys
stop being friends?"

"It's complicated," I said, scooting over a few boxes
labeled SUCTION CANISTERS. "Which is to say, I don't actually

know. She said I was boring, but I'm the same person I used to be and she liked me just fine before."

He was quiet for a minute and then said, "That is complicated."

I hadn't talked to anybody about it yet, because I definitely couldn't talk to Em about it, or the Lauras, and no way was I going to talk to my parents about it, and if I could not talk to Grandma Van about anything ever, that would be perfect. But it was kind of nice talking about it to Howe.

Too bad we were running late. "Can you help me with this?"

Together, we eased out the big cooler. It was a flashy Chicago Football cooler, and had about enough room for two heads. The other head would have to ride solo in the smaller cooler.

"Shotgun!" Lake yelled.

"Fabulous," McMullen mumbled.

Since we'd lost time tying up Em, I wasn't about to let them argue about who got which cooler: without any more discussion, I used some Hippocrates oven mitts I'd grabbed from home to pop the guys into the coolers, McMullen and Andy in the big cooler, and Lake in the little Styrofoam cooler with a picture of a walrus on one side. The walrus had a bow tie, a dopey smile, and a cartoon bubble that said NICE ICE.

"Oh. Do you need ice?" I asked. "I didn't think of that."

"No! No," Andy said. "We need to keep defrosting. It's a long process, you know."

"I don't know. I don't *want* to know," I said. "The only thing I want to know is if you need ice."

"Maybe if you have a little something to pour over the ice…" Lake suggested.

"Lake," Andy warned.

"Tyrant."

When I'd finished getting everybody packed, I turned to Howe, who was inspecting a plastic skeleton dangling in one corner of the lab. "Which one do you want?" I asked.

He let go of the plastic leg bone he'd been holding in the air. "Which what do I want?"

"Which cooler?"

He gave me a blank look.

"I am not dragging three heads all the way to this place by myself, Howe. I hereby amend the verbal contract so it states that you are required to carry a minimum of one head."

He sighed. "I'll do it, but see, you can't just amend the contract whenever you want to. This is exactly what my mom says is the problem with verbal contracts." He looked at the two coolers, then pointed to the smaller one. "I'll take that one."

"Fine. Keep it steady."

"Yes, please," Lake said from inside.

I put the lid on Lake and handed him to Howe. Then I

looked down into the big cooler. I could only see the tops of the heads, like two giant hairy eggs. "Okay in there?"

"Could be worse," Andy said.

"Hmmph," McMullen said.

I closed the lid, grabbed the handle, and rolled the big cooler out of the lab and down the Hall of Innards.

"Wait," said Howe, catching up to me. "That one has wheels?"

"No take-backs."

11:39 p.m.

"This is absurd."

We hadn't even gotten out of the lobby and Em was refusing to move. "I can't walk if I can't see."

"She's got a point." Howe had rested the small cooler on the desk and was retying both of his shoes.

"Of course I have a point," she said. "Maybe you should reconsider kidnapping somebody and making them be part of your secret club when they don't want to be a part of it."

"Are we talking about kidnapping again?" asked Lake from the cooler on the desk. "Can we revisit that Tiger Kidnapping business? And also, can I ask for a little more information about the secret club? Is there a handshake? Because—"

I hit the cooler and heard him thump against the side.

"Oh. Right. Never mind."

"Who said that?" Em asked, moving her head around like she was trying to find a spot I might have missed with the blackout marker.

"Everybody relax!" I said. "There's no kidnapping happening. We're just helping spice up Em's summer." It was going to be short-lived spice if I couldn't figure out how to get her to Nussbaum's.

"Too bad she doesn't have wheels," said Andy from inside the big cooler. "This is quite smooth, actually."

"A little crowded, though," said McMullen.

"WHO ARE THESE PEOPLE?"

"Em, this is the rest of Howe's barbershop quartet. Andy, Lake, and McMullen. Guys, this is my fr—this is Em."

She frowned. "Why do they sound so muffled?"

"They are . . ."

"We're singers!" said Lake from the walrus cooler. "We're just saving our voices."

We all waited a moment to see if Em was going to buy it.

"Hmm. Smart," she said.

How about that? I thought. The guys were actually being helpful. And suddenly I knew what to do about the problem of walking a blindfolded person fifteen blocks downtown.

11:42 p.m.

Outside in the warm night air, the rest of the gang waited for me to lock the door. Howe looked around nervously as he held Lake. Next to him was the large cooler with the other two guys inside, and Em, blindfolded and tied up with yarn and veggies, sitting on top of it.

We'd ridden horses at camp once. So okay, this wasn't really a horse. And she was riding backwards. She'd be fine. As soon as she stopped being angry, she'd be totally fine.

I pulled out the keys and tried not to second-guess myself. Once I locked the door and we walked away, there was no turning back. Or at least, turning back was going to be way more awkward. I held the key ring in the street-light to find the right key, and as I did, something a block away clattered. Howe and I both jumped, staring down the dark street.

Nothing. A few parked cars, a flickering streetlight. On the far side of the street, the stairs to the train platform were empty.

I looked to Howe and he shrugged slightly.

Midnight was closing in. It was definitely time to get moving.

I locked the door and we started the walk to Nussbaum's. Em and the heads were in the dark, literally, what with her being blindfolded and them being stuck inside coolers, but Howe and I stayed on the alert for any sort of lurking danger. I wished the cooler wasn't so creaky—it clearly wasn't made to carry people. Entire people, anyway. It probably would have been fine with just the heads. But having Em as a passenger meant that the wheels made a grinding noise as we went, and nothing I did seemed to make them roll quieter. We were about halfway down the block when Howe suddenly started walking faster. "What's wrong with you?" I asked, trying to keep up.

"Don't look," he said, "but I think we're being followed." I looked.

"I said *don't* look."

"I didn't see anything."

"I don't see anything either!" said Em from on top of the cooler. "Because, if you recall, you're making me wear this blindfold."

"I'm not being funny," said Howe.

"Neither am I," she said.

"I'm serious," he said, sounding rattled. "Don't talk. Walk. Look casual."

We walked, trying to move a little faster but at the same time appear as casual as a kidney and James Bond and a blindfolded vegetable stand on a cooler possibly could. As we crossed the street, Howe glanced behind us again. "Cheese it!" he cried, and bolted ahead of me.

"Cheese *what*?" asked Em, her question turning into a shriek as I yanked the cooler and started running. "Hold on!" I called back.

"WHAT! THE! HECK!" She'd flopped down onto her

stomach, and since she didn't have her arms free, was holding on with her legs.

Most of me was thinking: *RUN*, but I admit, there was also a part that went like this: If nothing else, this is definitely going to make Em realize that I have a lot of exciting stuff going on. I pulled the cooler as hard as I could, trying to close the distance between me and Howe, and Em let out a yell as one of the wheels jammed.

The jammed wheel made the cooler swerve erratically, and I had to jerk it forward with every running step while Em just kept saying, "WHAT. THE. HECK" over and over again. I finally caught up with Howe, who was definitely struggling with the too-tight elements of the tuxedo, and I could hear Lake thumping against the small cooler as Howe's feet hit the ground. This didn't look good for any of us.

We turned a corner, and Howe pulled us into the darkened entryway of a run-down old flower shop, fake daffodils still in the windows. I was so out of breath I wasn't sure how much longer I could have run. I dragged the cooler and Em against the door where the shadows were heaviest and whispered, "Quiet, everybody!"

I tried to breathe quietly. *Exist* quietly.

Standing beside me, Howe held the little cooler tight, and both of us shrank into the shadows. I hoped Em could stay quiet for a minute. And I hoped Howe was right, that by hiding like this, we'd lose whoever was following us. Because if he was wrong, we were now sitting ducks.

We pressed our backs against the front windows of the flower store, chameleoning ourselves into the dark. I am a flower, I thought. Nobody here but us daffodils. I tried to think over the deafening sound of my heart beating. Who would be following us? Inko Fredrickson? The police? A random mugger? Please let it be a random mugger, I thought. Random mugger was just hands down the best option. A random mugger would have no interest in what we were carrying.

I heard a noise. Danger had totally been lurking, and now it was lurking around the corner, turning the corner, heading right toward us with a low electric hum.

Danger stopped in front of us. Danger was in a motorized scooter, wearing all black, including a face mask that revealed no more than an extremely wrinkly forehead and a pair of drugstore eyeglasses. In the wire basket attached to the front of the chair was Grandma Van's purse and a box of crackers. The masked driver of the scooter looked around and, spotting us, froze.

What the heck, indeed.

"Grandma Van?" I asked.

The masked driver sighed a gravelly sigh.

17.

HIPPOCRATES
DID NOT RELY ON CRUD

11:47 p.m.

So the random mugger was, in fact, about as random as possible.

"Is your *grandma* in the club?" asked Em, her goggled face resting sideways on the cooler. "Seriously. This is the weirdest club."

"She is not in the club," I said sternly.

"You have a club?" Grandma Van asked. "What, a kidnapping club?"

"*Thank* you," said Em. "See, people? This is *clearly* a kidnapping. Mrs. De Leon, could you please untie me? I am currently the unwilling participant of some sort of weird club hazing, and frankly, I think Fovea is setting herself up for a life of crime with all this, so it's really in everybody's best interest—"

"Grandma Van, what are you doing here?" I asked, preferring to avoid the subject of kidnapping.

Grandma Van pulled the black face mask off, dropped it into the wire basket, and sighed again. "I'm not on some sort of pathetic elderly lockdown, just because I'm closing in on my dirt nap," she said. "I can leave the Swan Song whenever I like. All of us can."

"Her dirt nap?" Howe asked out of the side of his mouth.

"She's been gearing up to die for a long time," I explained.

"I'm pretty sure it's any day now," Grandma Van said.

"You look awfully spry to me," said Howe.

"You take that back," she said indignantly.

He glanced at me and I nodded. "I mean," he said politely, "you look like you're on your last leg."

"Thank you," said Grandma Van. "And that's your little friend Em riding behind you in the goggles and vegetables?"

Em huffed. "Little nothing. You may be older, but I'm still taller than you, Mrs. De Leon."

"Not all kidnapped like that you aren't," Grandma Van snorted.

I was glad they were getting along and all, but this was still a standoff. "Grandma Van, it's good to see you, but we need to be going."

"Oh, I don't think so," she said. "It's late, you kids shouldn't be out like this. We should all go back home. To bed."

"No!" I said, glancing at Em and the cooler of heads. My crackpot grandmother wasn't stopping me now. No, I was making this happen. Sure I wanted to turn back, but I couldn't do it until Em was having fun with me again and the stupid heads had gotten their stupid favor and my parents were saved. And none of that had happened yet.

"I've got this," Howe said under his breath. "I took a class."

"In arguing with people's grandmothers?" I asked.

"In being a negotiator. It was part of the Children's Refinement Undercover Detective class. How to be a spy. We learned a lot of valuable things. How to walk silently. How to use a shoe as a recording device. The only way to combat chaos is with more chaos."

"CRUD," observed Grandma Van. "Total CRUD."

"Well, no, it was pretty useful information," Howe said.

"It's an acronym. You said you learned it in a CRUD class. Children's Refinement Undercover Detective." She shook her head. "You know acronyms? I'll give you another example: HRHKHVIII."

"I'm sort of following you," Howe said diplomatically. "Almost."

I did not feel like this negotiation was going well. I

stepped in. "She's talking about His Royal Highness King Henry the Eighth. She's a big fan."

I guessed Howe knew a little something about all Henry VIII's murdering, both wife and non-wife, because his nervous hand went up to twist his hair, and he shifted the cooler into his other hand. As he did, he tipped it onto its side.

At which point Lake promptly started screaming.

I leapt for the cooler, set it upright in Howe's arms as quickly as I could, but I was too late. From inside, Lake said very clearly, "Oof. For goodness' sake, let's not do that again."

Grandma Van stared at the cooler. Howe and I stared at her. Everybody who was not blindfolded stared. I tried to think of anything to say, *anything*, because somebody was going to have to say something soon.

That somebody turned out to be Lake. His voice drifted out from the cooler. "Since there's a lull in the conversation, I'd like to say that I'm feeling just a bit claustrophobic. Also, something in here smells like mayo. Can I get a little air?"

That wasn't what I'd been hoping for.

Howe halfheartedly shushed him.

A streetlight buzzed. It flickered off and then on again.

Finally, Grandma Van spoke. "What is in there? And what *exactly* are *you* doing here, Fovea?"

"Oh. You know." If I could have melted into the sidewalk, I would have gladly done it at that moment. But at this point, the only way I could see out of the mess was straight on, driving right into the eye of the storm. It was going to be impossible to get past her otherwise. Unfortunately, the person who would have been perfect for dealing with this type of situation was tied up and blindfolded behind me, so I was going to have to make it work myself.

"Howe," I said, quickly examining the jammed cooler and pulling out a blue bit of plastic that had wedged itself against the wheel. "I need to have a private conversation with my grandmother. Would you take Em for a short walk?"

"I am not going anywhere!" Em declared, and vigorously tried to free herself, but only succeeded in shaking off a couple of radishes. They dribbled across the sidewalk and came to rest at one of Grandma Van's wheels. Howe carefully handed me the small cooler and rolled the big cooler, along with Em, down the sidewalk. As they left, Em announced, "This is, just to be super clear, the worst secret club in history."

"It will get more exciting," I called back, hoping that was true. "I mean, good exciting."

Howe was still shooting me warning glances over his shoulder, but I ignored him. He didn't understand: this had to happen. Grandma Van couldn't be distracted. She'd smell a distraction and go in for the kill. This was the only way.

As soon as I was sure they were out of earshot, I turned to

Grandma Van. "I have some bad news," I said. "It seems . . . that maybe death is a little . . . iffy."

Grandma Van looked at me suspiciously. "You don't know what you're talking about. I've already bought my pine condo. Paid in full. Just waiting to move in. Nothing iffy about that."

"I didn't make the rules," I said. "I barely understand them."

"The rules are simple, kiddo. Room temperature is coming to us all."

"Well," I said, bracing myself. "Maybe. But maybe not. I'm going to show you something, all right? This is for your eyes only. *You can't tell anyone.*"

I waited for her to agree, which she did. I hoped she meant it.

I took the top off Lake's cooler.

"Oh, much better!" said Lake as he peered out.

Grandma Van's jaw dropped.

"This is your grandmother, Fovea?" asked Lake. "A pleasure to meet you! Enchanted! Are you, by any chance, a patron of the arts?"

Grandma Van didn't respond. Her mouth was still open. I waved my hand in front of her face. It was like somebody paused her. I nudged her shoulder a little. Nothing. I hadn't expected nothing. I wasn't sure what to do, so I called Howe and Em back.

"I think you might have broken her," said Howe, after waving his own hand in front of her face.

"What's going on?" Em demanded. "In case you forgot, *I still can't see!*"

"She's just being . . . thoughtful," I said.

"That doesn't sound like her," said Em.

"She's turning over a new leaf. A sort of sudden leaf. And we have to go," I said to Howe. "We're already late."

"Well, we can't leave her here," he said.

"Can't we?"

11:52 p.m.

Finally, we were on the way again.

Once Howe had convinced me that it was uncool to leave in-shock Grandma Van there, I'd realized that bringing her with us would actually speed up the process. We put the small cooler into the wire basket, resting it gently on top of the purse. Howe and I hopped on the back of the scooter. With his long legs and arms, he could reach the control buttons, while I just held on to the rolling cooler's handle, pulling it after us. Em kept her spot on top of it. I'd been worried the whole Grandma Van thing would get us to Nussbaum's late, but now we were making great time.

"Sorry if I'm crowding you," I said to Howe. "My costume is a little bulky."

"It's okay," he said. "What is it, anyway? A jelly bean?"

"A left kidney," I said as we motored on.

"It was part of her parents' Halloween costume," Em explained loudly. "They plan something as a group every year, and every year Fovea chickens out. Last year, they went as kidneys and tried to get Fovea to be the spleen."

"The costume didn't fit," I said quickly.

"You could have made one that fit," said Howe, missing the point that I didn't want to be a spleen in the first place. Which is *not* the same as being a chicken, thank you.

"I don't really know how to make things."

"It's not that hard, you know," he said. "Making stuff. There's a Children's Refinement Independent Art class. We invent projects and then do them."

"Like what kind of projects?"

"Like I don't know. One time I sewed this T. rex, stuffed it, and then made a diorama of myself being eaten by it."

"ADORABLE," said Em. "But seriously, are you kidnapping me to Michigan or something? Aren't we there yet?"

"Soon," I said. "Soon. About ten more blocks." I was really ready for Em to go ahead and realize she was having fun.

"Gun it!" called out Lake. "You know, if that's a possibility."

"Let me see what I can do," said Howe.

"We should probably keep our voices down—" I started to say, but then Howe did, in fact, gun it, and the scooter choked and whiplashed us forward, zipping down the dark sidewalk, the night wind whistling around us. Em whooped, which seemed like a possible good sign. I gave Howe the directions I'd looked up earlier that day, and within a minute or two, we'd left the downtown I knew. We crossed over into another part of downtown: grungier, dingier. This wasn't offices or apartment buildings—it was bars and empty diners with flickering lights. It looked like this was where the city kept all its skeletons.

Hopefully, not real ones.

A girl has her limits.

12:04 a.m.

We rolled to a stop in front of an old, dirty two-story building. Warehouses on either side loomed over it.

The windows on the top floor had been completely postered over from the inside, and one floor down, the front door was covered, too—a lot of old band posters, layers and layers of them. Over the door, swinging slightly in the night breeze, a metal sign said: NUSSBAUM'S MUSICALARIUM.

I stepped off the chair and was about to go to the door when Grandma Van surprised us, breaking out of her petrified condition to say: "I'm all in."

"Grandma Van?" I asked nervously. Did her eye just twitch? If she was completely losing it, my mom was not going to be happy with me. "All in for what?"

"Whatever we're here to do," she said slowly. "I'm in. Is it a fight club? I can fight. A séance? I know dead people. Are you using that"—she pointed a crooked finger toward the small cooler—"for some kind of bait? Is it like that movie, where you're going to put it under somebody's pillow to scare them?"

"Ew," said Howe.

"Absolutely not!" came Lake's voice. "Unless we're talking those Egyptian sateen sheets, maybe a five hundred thread count. I wouldn't mind—"

"What is everybody talking about?" asked Em, shifting under the veggie yarn impatiently. "I honestly haven't understood a single word that anybody has said in the last two minutes."

"Tell them what we're doing," Howe said. "You'll have to sometime."

"We're doing a musical recording session," I announced to Em and Grandma Van. "And we have arrived."

"Well, let's get in there," Grandma Van said, grinning. She waved me closer and lowered her voice to a whisper. "I haven't felt this alive in years!"

Em didn't say anything, but she'd tilted her head a little to the side, like she was listening extra hard. I was starting to get her point about not being able to have an adventure without seeing anything. Then again, she hadn't even believed I could get her here, and I'd done that. Somehow, I'd give her the adventure she wanted.

I stepped up and pulled on the door, but it was locked. Howe and I poked around the area beside it, lifting edges of old posters until we found a bell. He pushed it and we waited to see if anything would happen.

After a few long minutes, we heard bolts turning on the inside, the door swung open, and a guy in a black T-shirt faced us. Sunglasses rested on his shaven head, like he might need them at any second despite the fact that it was the middle of the night. I wondered if I could get away with wearing sunglasses at the lab. Probably not. He opened the door wider. His muscles practically needed their own zip code.

A bouncer.

An actual bouncer. This was who my parents needed. Seriously, those muscles. He examined the three of us. I wished like heck I wasn't dressed like a kidney.

12:08 a.m.

"You're late," he said.

18.

HIPPOCRATES DID NOT FEEL SHY IN SURPRISING SOCIAL SITUATIONS

Howe stepped in after the bouncer. Then Grandma Van motored in, driving like a tank over the doorway, and I brought up the rear, dragging the big cooler with Em on top. The door shut behind me, and we were in a dark, narrow hallway. It was lined with posters, inches thick of them, which made the hallway seem even narrower. The almost too-sweet smell of something just on the edge of going rotten hung in the air. I followed the rest of them into a large dim room with a stage and a small checkered dance floor. Across the room stretched a deserted bar with a mirror behind it, and shelves lined with liquor bottles and glasses.

Aside from us, the place was dead empty. I stood on the edge of the dance floor, checking it all out, although honestly, I felt more like the bar was checking *me* out.

"Is this place a bar?" Howe asked nobody in particular. His voice echoed around the space. "We're underage. Some of us, anyway. I don't think we should be here."

"Ha! I haven't been in a bar in forever," said Grandma Van, and I turned in time to see her zoom straight behind the counter and start clanking around.

"Hey, no," the bouncer said, chasing after her. "You can't go back there."

"It's a *bar*?" asked Em, trying to see through the blindfold again. "We're in a *bar*? You kidnapped me to a bar?"

"Whoa, whoa, whoa. Is she kidnapped?" The bouncer almost skidded as he whipped around. "You can't be bringing kidnapped people into this establishment. We're a reputable place, here."

"I am! I am kidnapped! Why are you even asking? How is that not obvious? I'm tied up with vegetables and some kind of yarn that is getting a little scratchy, frankly, and I'M BLINDFOLDED. I would really appreciate it if you would untie me right now, whoever you are, because I am *not interested in this club.*"

I might have been in trouble had Em been anybody else. But Em made people nervous, and I could see that the bouncer was already weighing whether it was going to just be safer to leave her alone. I jumped in.

"She's not kidnapped! She's..." I reached for the right word. "Joking. She's the manager of the band. She likes to focus on the music, that's why she's blindfolded. She lets her other senses take over, you know."

"Kidnapped," said Em.

"Manager of the band," I said.

"Kidnapped," said Em.

"Kidnapped manager of the band?" I offered. I was banking on two things: first, that she wanted me to admit that she was kidnapped as badly as she wanted to actually be untied. And second, that she would never turn down a position of authority.

She nodded. "I'll take it."

I turned back to the guy, who threw his hands up.

"Are you the sound guy?" Howe asked him.

The bouncer laughed gently.

There was a click, and we heard a woman's voice come over the sound system. "I'm the sound guy," she said. I looked around the room and finally spotted a tinted window halfway up one of the walls. I waved a few fingers at it.

"Yeah," the voice boomed. "Up here. I'm Nussbaum. That's Dirk."

The bouncer nodded his head at me.

"I presume the four of you are the barbershop quartet?" She sounded a little bit bored. "We should go ahead and get started, seeing as how you're late. Who did I talk to today?"

I raised my hand. "That was me. And before we begin, I just wondered about your privacy policies?"

"As long as you've got money, I don't care who you are."

Whoops.

I looked toward the coolers and they were completely silent. Those turds. I could guarantee none of the guys had any money on them.

I glanced at Grandma Van, and discovered that she was staring approvingly at the bouncer. "Ahem," I said, wondering what exactly had happened to her brain while she was in shock. "Grandma Van, can we borrow a little cash?"

Still staring, she made a small flirty growl. I decided to run with it. I wiggled her purse out from underneath the cooler in the scooter's basket.

"Yes, we are good with money," I said to the tinted window. "I'll bring it to you?"

"Sure. And that manager, too."

Em stood, a kale ghost. "Finally," she said. "A little respect."

I hoped I hadn't created a monster. There was a fine line between Em being impressed with me and Em being impressed with herself.

"Take your time," said Grandma Van, waving us on. "Dirk, young man, come tell me about your educational background."

"Keep an eye on my grandmother?" I whispered to Howe. He nodded nervously. We both knew it was an impossible job.

With me guiding her, Em and I made our way to the door and carefully up the stairs. They were steep, and I let her go first so I could catch her if she tripped. We were halfway to the top when she stopped. "Fovea?"

Not until she said it did I realize that this was the first time we'd been alone together since That Day. She's going to apologize, I thought, hope filling my cells like oxygen. This is it. "Yeah?"

"Don't you think it would be more convincing that I'm the manager if I'm not tied up?" she said.

My cells breathed out.

"I'll think about it," I told her. It was too soon, but at least she wasn't complaining anymore.

Nussbaum called down, "You kids get lost? We don't have all night here. Let's go, let's go."

The room at the top of the stairs was tight. It had a single large window on one wall, the one that we'd seen from the bar. On the bar side, the glass was tinted, but on this side you could see through it, and the height gave us a clear view of the whole room spread out below. The rest of the space was filled with equipment, each one with a little green or red light that blinked. In the middle of it all sat Nussbaum.

She was on a stool, one leg hitched up so she could tap impatiently on it. She wore cowboy boots and had three-foot-tall hair. Rings covered every one of her fingers. She looked like she might be the ruler of a small country of rock musicians.

"I'm Nussbaum," she said, sticking out her hand for me to shake. "That's an interesting . . . outfit."

"I'm a left kidney. My name is Fovea and this is Em."

Nussbaum reached out to shake Em's hand, but since Em couldn't see her hand and also didn't have a free hand herself, it sort of fizzled.

"Good evening," said Em, professional and oblivious at the same time.

I handed over Grandma Van's credit card, and as Nussbaum scanned it with a little swipe of her phone, I looked around, spotting a whole rack of headphones. Perfect.

"We need to talk business," I said to Nussbaum. "But maybe our, um, manager here could listen to something else you've recorded? So she knows your, um, style?" I wasn't sure style was a thing in recording music, but it sounded legit. Nussbaum looked at Em skeptically, but stood and grabbed a set of headphones. In a minute, Em was listening to something—something good, apparently, because she was jamming out.

Nussbaum sat back down on the stool and looked at me expectantly. Boy, did she not expect this.

"So we're okay?" I said. "With the privacy policy?"

"Sure, kid. Now let's get moving. What do you need, four mics? Is the vegetarian manager singing, too?"

"No, actually. Neither am I, neither is my grandmother. You should probably meet the other guys. Can you turn on that overhead PA system again?"

Nussbaum looked skeptical, but she hit a button and I heard the click.

"Howe," I said, startled at the sound of my voice suddenly everywhere. "Howe, can you please introduce Nussbaum to the guys?"

He gave us a thumbs up, and then made for the football cooler. I crossed my fingers as Howe grabbed the edges of the lid and opened it. I was really counting big time on that privacy policy.

"Well, hello," I heard Andy say.

"Can somebody get me out of here?" growled McMullen. We couldn't see them properly at this angle, but before I could tell Howe to tilt the cooler, Grandma Van drove her chair closer, directly in the way. "Oho!" she said. "Two more!"

"Sorry about my grandmother," I said. I pointed down

at the cooler. "You can't quite see them, but that's Andy and McMullen."

"Where?" Nussbaum asked, trying to get a better view.

It was tough because Grandma Van was now leaning out of her scooter, directly over the cooler. "You got chopped, too, huh," she was saying. "It's an epidemic! A neck-idemic!"

I thought I heard Lake laughing from inside the small cooler.

"I can't quite ..." Nussbaum stepped close to the glass.

Andy's voice came from the big cooler. "I prefer the term 'abbreviated at the neck,' ma'am."

"Call me Van."

"Van."

She smiled, patting down her hair, and leaned back. Dirk took her place, peering in, and one second later, we all watched as the giant bouncer wobbled and then slowly toppled over. Even through the thick glass, we could hear the loud *thump* as he ate it, right onto the checkered dance floor.

"What did they do to Dirk?" Nussbaum asked angrily.

"Nothing." I watched as Howe tried to help, but clearly found even Dirk's arms too heavy to lift. "He just met the other guys."

"*What* other guys?"

"They're down there. Just kind of low profile," I said.

I clicked on the PA system again. "Howe, will you show Nussbaum the guys? We don't have such a good view."

Howe obliged, tipping the cooler slightly so she could see. "They don't have bodies," he explained.

"*Convenient*," emphasized McMullen, his face pressing against the side of the tilted cooler. "We don't have bodies *convenient*. We have them, they just aren't around."

Nussbaum shook her head and stepped closer to the window. Then, without a word, she brushed past me, through the door, and down the stairs. I shot Em a quick glance and left her listening to whatever was on the headphones, racing down after Nussbaum.

Back in the bar, things had deteriorated somewhat.

Nussbaum was already standing over the cooler with her hands on her hips, and Howe was running between her and Grandma Van, trying, I discovered, to keep my grandmother from harassing the unconscious bouncer.

"Those sure are some muscles," Grandma Van was saying philosophically. "Just let me have a pinch."

"I don't think that's a good idea," Howe said, his arms out to block her. Hopefully, she wouldn't rush him. Letting him handle that situation for a minute, I turned my attention to Nussbaum. I wasn't sure she'd blinked yet.

"Hello," Andy said, looking up out of the cooler.

Nussbaum nodded back at him.

"You're still going to do it, right?" I asked. "The recording?"

"Well, you already paid."

Whew.

"Though I believe..." she said, looking back down into the cooler. "I believe you're going to need a few stools."

The two coolers rested on the edge of the stage, tops off, and Howe sat next to them, dangling his legs. Nussbaum paced in front and they all talked about the plan for the recording session.

That left me and Grandma Van to take care of the unconscious bouncer a few feet away.

"You should get up," she said to him. He didn't move. She nudged him a little with her scooter. Nothing. She leaned toward his face and said loudly, "Just think, we could rob this place blind if we wanted to."

The conversation in front of the stage went silent.

"Ummm..." said Nussbaum.

Grandma Van shrugged innocently. "I was trying to inspire him."

Nussbaum attempted a small smile and then they went back to figuring out the details. I wasn't sure it was the best idea, but I left Grandma Van with passed-out Dirk while I made my way behind the bar and grabbed a glass. As I ran water into it, I realized you could see the whole room from back there: the old wooden stage, the worn-down dance floor, the little round tables scattered here and there. For a dirty old bar, the place was kind of cool. Something about the way the dim light fell over everything. And how quiet it was, too, except for the low conversation on the edge of the stage. Maybe most of all, though, it was the way there was a promise inside the building that Something Was Going To Happen.

I was excited, despite everything.

I brought the glass of water over to Dirk and poured a little on his face, accidentally letting some roll into his nose. He woke up gasping. "Heads! They're heads!"

Grandma Van nodded. "It does throw a bit of a curveball into things, doesn't it?"

He glanced toward the stage, going pale again as Lake yelled, "Let's get this party started!" Dirk did not look ready to party. He put a shaky hand to his damp forehead and closed his eyes. "How many?"

"Of the guys? Three."

"Where are their bodies?" His voice wavered.

"Great question!" said Grandma Van with delight. "Just fantastic, right?"

Dirk shuddered.

"On the upside," I said, "they turn out to be pretty good singers."

"My goodness. Decapitated *and* melodious," murmured Grandma Van, motoring around us and going to join the gang by the stage.

"All right, folks," Nussbaum announced. "We've got a plan. Mics up?"

"Sounds good," Dirk said weakly.

"You get used to it," I whispered.

He nodded like he didn't, not for one second, believe me.

Once he had something to focus on, Dirk seemed a little sturdier. He got to work, setting up the front edge of the stage with towel-cushioned stools and microphones and black cables that snaked around his ankles.

I followed Nussbaum back to the small room, explaining as we went that Em could absolutely not see the heads. I lied and said that Em might freak out. I definitely *didn't* mention that I wanted her to have fun without considering me an Igor. Thankfully, Nussbaum bought my explanation, and when we got into the room, she set Em, still blindfolded, next to her stool. "I'm going to talk you through this recording with the blindfold still on," she said to Em, "so you can concentrate on the music."

Em seemed to consider it. "Okay."

Nussbaum and I nodded over her head, and then I went back downstairs to help. I really couldn't expect anybody else to do the dirty work.

We went fast. Howe found a spot onstage while I popped on the oven mitts and placed the heads on the stools, one by one. Dirk followed behind me, setting each person's microphone to stool/head level, and pulling the glasses down from the top of his head for the up-close adjustments. Huh. They weren't sunglasses at all. They were *reading* glasses.

While we were doing all the prep, Grandma Van slowly drove her chair back and forth in front of the stage telling a story about the time she saw Elvis Presley live when he played once in Manila. I'd never heard her talk about the past before. I'd really never heard her talk about anything other than her impending death and her nemesis, Julia Klinger. This was blowing my mind. "Sure, Elvis was handsome," she was saying, "but that night, he sounded flat, on every single song. The moral of the story is: you can't get away with just being good-looking."

"Thank you," said Lake.

"You were also a singer in your youth? Or a musician?" Andy asked her as I settled him onto his stool.

"I was more of a critic," said Grandma Van. "I find that people in the world need to be told what to think, more often than not."

Howe started to twist his hair, and I didn't blame him. I was a little worried, too. Grandma Van was veering toward a menace-to-society mood. I changed the subject. "So what are you guys going to call the barbershop quartet?"

That turned out to be a perfect distraction, since everybody had plenty of opinions. They still hadn't picked a name when Dirk and I finished, but they went ahead and started warming up with the microphones. They didn't need me anymore, so I went to the back, where there were stools against the wall.

Onstage, there was a sound check and a little practicing. Grandma Van asked to use the bathroom. Dirk pointed the way. For the first time all night, everything felt pretty calm. Thank goodness.

Several microphone tests later, Dirk came over to chill on a stool near me, and then Nussbaum announced that she was going to bring up some color to help with the atmosphere. Suddenly there were lights on the stage, dreamy blue and red splashes of colored light that caught all the dust in the air and bounced off the guys, making them look almost young. Healthier. Not recently deep-frozen and thawed. Howe didn't look so bad either.

But it didn't just change the four of them. The whole bar instantly felt different. The moment the lights hit the stage, everything was *more*. More interesting. Realer. Bigger. Even me, back there in the dark, dressed as a kidney. I wished Em could see it all, not just because it was so incredible, but because I wanted, so badly, to be in that magically cool experience *with* her.

It could be like it had been at the hologram museum.

Us standing side by side, thinking the same thing and not even having to talk about it. I wanted that back.

Removing the blindfold was completely off the table, of course, on account of the guys being out and about. It may have worked for the original Igor, but I was definitely not mixing fun and the transportation of body parts. We just have to get through this first, I told myself.

"That's what I'm talking about," Lake said from onstage, smiling and closing his eyes against the light, almost as if he was going to lean all the way into it. Oh no. He was. He was leaning into it.

"Lake!" I yelled, jumping up from the stool and just about giving Dirk a heart attack. "You'll tip over!"

Lake wobbled for a moment and then caught himself. "Thanks, Fovea! Close call!" With a glance sideways at the other guys, he said, "I have this sneaking suspicion I might not be cut evenly on the bottom. Anybody else ever feel like that? No?"

And then they began.

The three heads and Howe: they were like any other band now, the four of them, lined up onstage in the pools of light, singing their hearts out. And they looked so happy. All that time planning it in the body freezer, working out the details while chilling between the stacks of arms and legs and whatever. And the work I did, calling places and finding Howe. It was all paying off. Even Grandma Van clapped with surprising enthusiasm.

I realized this was the promise of Nussbaum's Musicalarium.

THIS was the thing that was Happening. And I was part of it. I was the reason it had happened at all.

It felt incredible. I realized that maybe, if I looked at it in a certain light, Em had been right, at least so far in my life. Maybe she wasn't being mean. Maybe she was calling it like it was. I *had* been boring. I *hadn't* done anything. Maybe I was a bookmark, holding on to a space and waiting for the right time.

And this, this was the time.

If I overlooked the fact that the heads were currently gooping up some barstools that could never be used again, everything was going really, really well. The guys seemed to be getting more used to each other as they went along, and every song got tighter, seemed to be better than the last.

They were nearly done when my pocket started vibrating.

I reached into the costume, pulled Whitney's phone out, and the screen glowed bright in the dark. Unknown was calling. Unknown! *Whitney!* I looked around to see where I should answer it. Dirk pointed me toward the door, so I smothered the phone against my stomach and ran outside.

"Hello!" I answered. "Whit—"

I didn't get any further because of the great amount of honking and snorting on the other end of the phone. It didn't sound like Whitney at all. It sounded like a man. A blubbering man. "You're on your way, right?" cried the blubbering man. "I can't stand the suspense! All this waiting! Are you on the way, Whitney?"

Crud. I turned the phone off. Inko was losing his cool.

And if Inko was losing his cool, then I might already be out of time. I needed to make sure the missing head was back in place. I needed to end this. I'd been so distracted by the guys and Howe and having Em around, but there wasn't time to be distracted anymore.

I turned and pushed into Nussbaum's again.

Back on my stool, I watched without really watching, thinking how the sooner the recording was done, the sooner we could get back to the lab, do whatever celebrating they wanted to do. Then I could find out where the other head was, and this could be over.

19.

HIPPOCRATES DID NOT CARE FOR SCENIC ROUTES

"I can't believe you missed it," Lake was saying as I lowered him into his cooler. Or that's what I deduced he said. One of my oven mitts was smushing his mouth.

Howe was trying not to be too obvious about keeping an eye on Grandma Van as she followed Dirk around while he took down the microphones and rolled the cables. We'd discussed it, and somebody needed to protect the bouncer. Nussbaum and Em were still up in the little room.

I settled Lake in and moved on to Andy. "I only missed like five minutes."

Lake sighed dramatically. "But it was an *outstanding* five minutes."

"It's perfectly all right, dear," said Andy.

McMullen appeared to be napping. When I picked him up, he yawned and blinked a few times.

I put the lids on the coolers, and the place suddenly felt hollow. The stage lights were off and the whole bar seemed colder, emptier than it had when we'd first gotten there. All that promise had been spent.

I collected Em from the upstairs room, despite the fact that she didn't want to go. "We can't go yet! I have so many more questions! We only covered the basics! How am I supposed to be a good manager if don't know whether to remix or lay down the tracks as they are?" We set her on the cooler again as she talked about EQ adjusting and made our way back outside, where she went on about sound balance something or other. I was glad she was finally having fun, even if I didn't understand a word she was saying. And right then, I didn't really have time to figure it out. I had a lovesick cremator to neutralize.

Out on the sidewalk, it was still dark.

Dirk appeared just as Howe and I were stepping onto the back of Grandma Van's chair. He held out a flash drive. "From Nussbaum," he said, taking the reading glasses off his head. "And for what it's worth . . ." He used the glasses to scratch behind an ear.

I waited for him to finish his sentence.

But he didn't. He waved the glasses toward the coolers, then at Grandma Van, all the while shaking his head. Then he looked at me, gave a single nod, and he and all his muscles disappeared into the Musicalarium.

I stared after him until Grandma Van beeped the horn on the scooter. Em was still talking about what she'd learned, but I kept playing back that last moment with Dirk. He was *impressed* with me. Right? I wasn't making that up? I climbed on next to Howe, snagged the corner of the kidney on the chair briefly, and then pulled free. Grandma Van revved the scooter and we took off into the dark morning.

"Almost home," I said, more to myself than anybody else. "Just a few blocks."

There was a brief pause and then, from her perch on the rolling cooler, Em said, "Locks."

"Rocks," I answered automatically.

It was nothing big or important. Just a dumb rhyming game we used to play at the drama camp. But in an instant, it was like nothing had broken between us at all. A few random rhyming words, filling me with the rush of what it had been like when we were one whole thing. Those dumb rhymes felt more important to me than any actual conversation we could possibly have had at that moment.

"Shocks," she said.

"Knocks."

"International peace talks," offered Howe.

"Diabetes compression socks," threw out Grandma Van.

"Necks!" called Lake, longingly.

Em burst out laughing and I couldn't stop smiling as we bumped down the sidewalk. Everything felt *right*.

At least, it did until Howe looked past me. "We're going the wrong way."

"Grandma Van?" I said, alarmed. "This isn't the way—we came from that direction."

"Surprise!" she said, glancing over her shoulder. "I decided we're taking the scenic route!"

"Noooooo. We don't need scenic. A regular route will be fine," I said quickly. *"We don't have time."*

She waved me off. "There's time. You need to live a little. I think 'All Scenic, All the Time' might be my new motto. And the fellas, no offense, are getting a little rank. I think we should air them out before the big party."

"There's a party, too?" asked Em.

"How do you know about the party?" I asked Grandma Van.

"The world moves in mysterious ways," she said. "As you may have recently noticed."

"She spied on us in the lab," Howe said.

"I did no such thing," she said, "and how did you find out?"

He mumbled.

"Speak up! Or don't say anything at all!" Then she added thoughtfully, "That also might be my new motto."

"In my Children's Refinement Undercover Detective class—"

"In which class?" she asked pointedly.

He sighed. "In my CRUD class, we learned how to identify the weak elements of a plan," Howe said. "That was a weak element. We weren't watching our backs during that conversation."

Something still didn't make sense to me. "But why'd you stalk us like that?"

"You said you were going to be doing something dangerous," she said, exasperated. "I'm your grandmother, Eyeballs. It's part of my job to protect you from dangerous things. If I was the king of England, it would be easier to just stop people from doing things I don't like, but as I have discovered with the whole Julia Klinger situation, I don't seem to have that kind of pull. So I was just going to tail you. I didn't mean for you to see me."

I was so stunned that I couldn't think of anything to say. Since when did Grandma Van look out for me? Then again, I'd never done anything dangerous before.

And then we turned a corner and I understood why this was the scenic route. I also completely forgot about the grandmotherly stalking. And pretty much everything else.

Suddenly all I could see in front of us was starlit Lake Michigan, endless and watery, dressed up like the edge of the world.

"All right!" Grandma Van's voice seemed to go on forever now that we were out in the open. She came to a stop on the lake path, which stretched out in either direction, just as empty as the streets had been. The path lay between the city and the lake, the border of the abyss. "Let's get reorganized!" She snapped her fingers. Howe and I glanced at each other.

"Reorganized how?" I asked.

"Well, it's no good being scenic if half the people can't see, is it?"

"Does this mean it's time for me to take off the blindfold?" asked Em.

"Nope," I said. "Not, um, you."

She growled. But a little more nicely than before.

A few minutes later, we were moving again. I was still pulling the rolling cooler behind the scooter, but it was a lot lighter now.

"Stop leaning so hard!" growled McMullen.

"I'm doing my best!" said Andy.

"Just think about being light as a feather," Lake cooed.

"Easy for you to say," said McMullen. "You've got the best spot."

"Guys," I said. "Remember what I said about certain topics of conversation?" I didn't want Em to start trying to picture what was going on.

Grandma Van had her purse in her lap now. She'd thrown the box of crackers in a nearby trash can. That left exactly enough room in her wire basket for the three heads. They were jumbled in there, free and open for anyone to see. Anyone who wasn't blindfolded. McMullen got the short straw, so he was on the bottom. Andy was in the middle, leaning slightly to one side, and Lake was on top of him, leaning in the opposite direction. "I've been meaning to get a new basket anyway," Grandma Van said when I mentioned the biohazard issue. "I want one you can't see through. I value my privacy more than some of those other old coots, and that way people can't tell if I have the Taser on me."

"Taser?" I asked, not sure I heard her right. Except *of course* I heard her right. Ugh. "You have a *Taser?*"

"I borrowed one from a lady down the hall from me. I wasn't sure what the night was going to bring."

Boy, did I get that.

"This is splendid, Van," Andy said. "Just splendid."

"Well, hell, I always wanted a real sidecar," said

Grandma Van, clearly pleased with herself. "This is pretty close. I'll call it a frontcar."

"We're like Thelma and Louise!" said Lake. "And Louise and Louise."

"I don't believe there was a sidecar in that movie," said Andy. "Or, er, a frontcar."

"There definitely was," argued Lake.

"I've seen a lot of movies," Andy said.

"Maybe your time on ice got you confused."

"*My* time?" Andy said indignantly.

"Guys!" I said.

"Hey," grumbled McMullen from the bottom of the pile. "The more you talk, the heavier you get. I'm no Bobby-Duran, here."

"Who's Bobby-Duran?" asked Howe.

He paused. "This guy I knew. Real strong. *Almost* became 1996 West Side Bowling Champion. Except he started throwing the ball too hard. You don't have to be strong to bowl, but it helps. Helps right up until—"

"Can we go any faster?" I interrupted. "Didn't we go faster earlier?"

"You know, kid, you should really stop trying to zoom through life so quick. Look around. Appreciate stuff. Be grateful for the splendors of nature." Then Grandma Van hawked a loogie and sailed it over the heads.

We chugged on into the dark morning.

Too freaking slow.

To our left, the water was shuffling up against the shore and then wandering away again, like it was totally not impressed by the sight of a scooter with two kids clinging to the back, one kid pulled behind it, and a frontcar full of heads.

Heads, by the way, that *were still defrosting.* They were clearly getting saggier in the face, and I couldn't stop hearing the slow *drip drip drip* from the bottom of the basket. Another reason to get back to the A/C blast of the lab. And if anything, it seemed like we were going slower.

Some kind of night bug landed on the belly of the kidney costume and I watched as it paced drunkenly, like it was tracing my intestines underneath. I thought about my parents, hopefully asleep in their beds.

Almost there, I thought to them. By tomorrow morning, you'll have all four heads again, and you won't know about any of this. We're almost there.

Right about then, the scooter came to a sudden and unexpected stop.

20.

HIPPOCRATES
DID NOT GET OUT
AND PUSH

It took me a second to realize that we weren't just stopping for Grandma Van to admire something or, equally likely, hawk a loogie onto it.

"Well, dang," she said. "I guess that's that."

A wave crashed nearby, invisible in the darkness.

"That's what, Van dear?" asked Andy.

"That's the end of my battery life. Well, I should be clear. Ha! Not MY battery life. The *scooter's* battery life."

She cackled quietly and we all sat in the mostly dark,

infinitely still. On one side of us, tall office buildings loomed. On the other side, the lake shushed against the shore.

"This seems inconvenient," said Andy.

"It's no problem," Grandma Van said. "I just flip this switch and then it's on manual. We'll have the young people push the rest of the way. It isn't far."

"Sorry," I mumbled to Howe as we stepped off the chair.

"It's okay," he said. "At least we're close."

He was right, but suddenly I was so tired. He pushed the chair and I kept pace alongside it, pulling the cooler and Em, leaning into each step like I was falling forward, endlessly, and using the cooler to keep me from going all the way down. I glanced back at Em, at the ropes of garlic tied around her, the assorted other vegetables swinging with the motion of driving along the path. I wanted to be friends again. I wanted it so badly, it hurt to even think about it straight on.

The grassy areas on either side of the path expanded and we started passing wooden posts, probably to keep people off the grass. Every three steps, another wooden post, regular, like a clock, ticking to remind me that time was running out.

Grandma Van narrated the trip for Em, but I ignored her until she finally said, "Hang a left! Here's where we jog back into the city."

"Scenic time is over," I said, starting to stow the guys

away again, but there was a lot of arguing, and frankly, I didn't have the strength to argue with anybody anymore. So we compromised, reentering the city with a lap blanket draped over the wire basket. I could feel the lab pulling on me like a magnet. All I had to do was get us a few more measly blocks, hang a few measly streamers so that we could call it a party, and then I'd get the missing head back and my parents would be in the clear. That was all.

Break it down, like my dad said.

It was feeling totally doable.

And then we turned the corner. We stopped right in our tracks and stared at what lay before us.

The line snaked down the sidewalk, and people stood in huddles of threes and fours and fives, some of them on scooters, or with walkers, or just freestanding. I gasped.

"What?" asked Em. "What is it?"

"Senior citizens," I said. "There must be hundreds of them. Waiting in a line that goes all the way to the front door of the lab."

"Very surprising," Grandma Van agreed.

"It's after two in the morning," I said. "How are they still awake?"

"Oh no, they're *already* awake. We get up early, see."

Wait a minute.

"Did you do this?" I asked her.

"Oh yes."

"WHY?"

She threw her hands in the air, all innocent. "I did what your mother told me, that's all."

"My *mom* told you to bring the entire population of the Swan Song to the cadaver lab in the middle of the night? That doesn't sound like her, Grandma Van."

"Well, I believe your mother's actual words were: 'Try something new.' So when we were at Nussbaum's, I put in a quick call to the Swan Song while I was in the bathroom. You know..." She lowered her voice to a whisper. "Julia Klinger thinks she's so fancy, but she has never once thrown a destination party."

"This is what happens when you have weak elements in your plan," Howe said, shaking his head. "Most *successful* plans are airtight."

"Most *grandmothers* do not spy, become completely unhinged, and plan secret location revenge parties," I replied.

"Most plans don't have you-know-whats," Howe pointed out.

"Recording sessions?" asked Em.

"Yes," said me, Howe, and Andy all at the same time.

"Can we all please focus on what's important here?" Grandma Van said, patting her hair. "We're about to throw the party of the century."

21.

HIPPOCRATES
DID NOT GET
TERROR-FIED

Groups of things have names, you know. Like how you have a Flock of Turkeys or a Murder of Crows or an Ostentation of Peacocks, that sort of thing. We covered that in sixth-grade English, in one of those fluffy mini-chapters, the ones called "Language: Spice Up Your Life."

I was pretty sure that the group I was currently looking at should be called a Terror of Old People.

Three buses with the Swan Song insignia waited by the curb up ahead, motors running. They must've made multiple trips to get this many people here. I started to sweat. "Why did you invite so many of them?"

"Well, I just told my neighbor Victoria to spread the word. I didn't do an RSVP or anything. Boy, she spread the word all right." She whistled. "Must've been a slow night at the Swan Song."

"How many people? How many exactly?" asked Lake from under the lap blanket.

"About a million," I said.

"I want to see," said Em. "Hey, Lake Michigan—"

"It's just *Lake*."

"I'll give you twenty bucks if you untie me."

Grandma Van snorted.

"That's probably not going to happen, my dear," said Andy.

"I'll just describe them for you," said Howe. "They are old and they are everywhere."

"It's going to be a tight fit in there, but we'll manage," Lake said. "We can also open the patio."

"What patio? There is no patio," I said. "It's a *cadaver lab*."

"Well, the back alley. But I bet it could be delightful. Just needs the right touch."

We watched them all for a minute, unseen, and then Grandma Van said, "What are we waiting for?"

I desperately tried to think of something to wait for.

"Let's go!" Lake cried.

"So many of them," Howe said as we started moving. "So many old people."

Grandma Van waved here and there like a queen. "Shh," she said under her breath. "They don't like it when you call them old. They prefer 'mature.'"

"That's a lot of extremely mature people," Howe said.

"Better," said Grandma Van.

We continued until we'd made our way to the front of the line, where, directly in front of the door, with her arms crossed, was an old lady wearing a small hat decorated with fake grapes. Aside from the hat, everything else she was wearing was drenched in sequins. She eyed us as we approached, and a chilly silence fell as I dug in my backpack for the keys.

"Julia," said Grandma Van icily.

"Vanessa," said the woman, matching her tone of voice.

"So good of you to come TO MY PARTY," Grandma Van said, loud enough for the front half of the line to hear.

"Oh, look, I found the keys," I said.

"I wouldn't MISS IT," Julia said, ignoring me.

Grandma Van fanned herself with a hand. "We just have to do a few last-minute preparations, if you'll excuse us?"

"By all means," said Julia. "I'll be interested to see what you're able to cook up. My expectations, you should know, are low."

"Ooh, snap," said a feebly heckling old man a little way behind them.

"Oh, look, the door's open now," I said.

Julia finally noticed me, which didn't feel like a win. "Why's your granddaughter dressed like a poo?" she asked disdainfully.

"It's a kidney," I said weakly.

"You sure did get here early, to be first in line," Grandma Van snarled. "It's almost like you *want* to be here."

"I drove," Julia said. "*I* still have my license."

"Should have been revoked years ago! Every time you get behind that wheel, you're a danger to all living things," Grandma Van hissed.

"She's jealous of my ride is all," sneered Julia Klinger. "1959 Cadillac Miller-Meteor, bought it in Ypsilanti eight years ago." She wiggled her eyebrows at Howe, who had slipped away from behind the scooter and was trying to become one with the wall.

"I don't know much about cars," he said weakly.

"It's not a car! It's a *hearse*! Another example of the decline of your generation," she said looking down her nose at him.

"Oh, look, here we go," I said, pulling Howe back into place so he could push the scooter and Grandma Van safely inside before an actual physical brawl could break out. Then I spun around to pull Em in after me, thankful at least that the elderly drama had distracted people from asking about the tied-up girl on top of the cooler.

Before I could pull the cooler in, though, Julia tapped me on the shoulder. "You sure you want to get behind that old horse? She's a born loser. And this party is going to suck all the wind out of two hundred and fifty old windbags, which is a lot of wind. Why don't you join me, huh? I have some great ideas for activities that could involve young people. Recycling. Synchronized dancing in lines. That sort of thing. You'll think about it, won't you?"

I looked at her and at the grapes bouncing on her head. I shook my head. "Sorry."

She didn't know it yet, because she hadn't met the new, fired-up-to-be-alive Grandma Van, but she was about to go down.

The line behind her was on the verge of getting rowdy, and I realized that I had an excellent solution to the rowdiness. "Em? Um . . . I'm going to unblindfold you now."

"SERIOUSLY?" she asked from her spot on the cooler. "We go to a bar and all sorts of cool stuff happens and then you take off the goggles *when the old people arrive*?"

"Yeah . . ." I carefully pulled the goggles off her head and then, while she blinked a bunch, I started to unwind the vegetables. "It's a pretty impressive amount of old people, though, right?"

"I guess," she said, looking down the line.

"So, I have to go inside for a minute," I said. "Will you make sure they don't break anything?"

"Like, break a window or break a hip?"

"Um, either. And in exchange—I'll let you go into the lab without the goggles on."

"You promise?"

Oh boy. "I promise."

She nodded. As I slipped inside and locked the door behind me, I wondered how I was ever going to make this whole thing happen.

Moments later, the rest of us stood (or were placed) in the middle of the wet lab and stared down at the pathetic pile of streamers I'd brought. The three blue rolls were left over from a science fair project I did in third grade about deoxygenated blood. A few hours ago, they'd just looked old; after spending hours at the bottom of my backpack, they were old *and* smushed.

Howe unzipped his fanny pack and pulled out a can of bean dip. He set it on the operating table next to the streamers. This party was not going to impress the mature people.

Grandma Van clearly agreed. "Well, this isn't what I was thinking at all. When I overheard you talking about throwing a party in a cadaver lab, I assumed the point of the party would be *looking at cadavers*," she said. "This is sort of a letdown."

"We are NOT showing them cadavers," I said firmly.

"They'll be so disappointed."

"That's not my problem. I wasn't the one who invited the whole Swan Song. That was your idea."

"Fine. I guess streamers and bean dip is fine. That dip isn't going to last too long, though. They love soft foods."

"I've been known to do wonders with streamers," said Lake. "Just so everyone knows."

Howe's hand went up in the air and Grandma Van called on him. "Yes, young man?"

He reached in the fanny pack again. "Here's the drive with everything we recorded tonight. We've got music—so it could be a dance party."

"Not a bad idea," she said.

I poked one of the crepe-paper rolls. Two hundred old people hanging out in a cadaver lab. There was a joke in there somewhere, but before I could think of it, an idea hit me. "Or you could sing live."

"What?" said Andy.

"Whoa," said McMullen.

"Brilliant!" said Lake.

"No way," said Howe.

"What's the problem?" Grandma Van asked, smiling big. "That is a *great* idea."

"Some, er . . . logistics issues," said Andy.

"I am ON IT," said Lake with enthusiasm. "This is going to be my masterpiece!"

"Maybe it doesn't have to be the whole quartet?" Howe said, shifting uncomfortably. "I, uh, should probably be going home soon."

Lake snorted. "There's no such thing as a barbershop trio."

Howe shot me a worried look. "Can we chat in the hallway?"

"Don't worry about us!" said Lake. "We'll be the decoration committee!"

I wasn't sure how much decorating the three guys and Grandma Van could accomplish, but we left them to brainstorm and ducked into the Hall of Innards.

"I don't really have to do this, do I?" He was getting sweaty. "It's—it wasn't in the contract."

"*This* is what you have a problem with? Because pretty much *everything* we've done tonight wasn't in the contract."

"But you promised there wouldn't be an audience."

"I did?" I could barely remember what we'd said. It seemed like lifetimes ago.

"I'd just really rather do anything else."

"Than perform? You don't like performing?"

He twisted himself up for a second and then, letting out a giant breath, said, "I have massive stage fright."

"You're a singer and you don't like performing?" I

needed him to sing. "But I saw you perform, in school. In that chorus assembly."

"I had to. It was for a grade. It was the worst day of my life."

"The worst day of *your* life?"

"Um, yeah."

I clapped my hand over my mouth.

"What?" he said. "It's not funny."

"I'm not laughing at you," I said. "That's not it. It was the worst day of my life, too."

"Because of the assembly? We were that bad?"

"No," I couldn't believe he didn't know. "Howe, haven't you heard people at school calling me Igor? Like Frankenstein's Igor?"

"That's *you*?"

I nodded.

"I guess it does make sense," he said after a second.

"Way too much sense after tonight," I agreed. "So we both had a bad day. But you've performed before. It's not like that was your first time. All those assemblies over the years. And what about the puppet show?" The moment it was out of my mouth I regretted it. Things had been going so well.

"What puppet show?" he asked, glancing at the ceiling, like he was trying to remember. "Actually maybe I should just—"

"Do you seriously not remember it? *Who What When Where You?*"

"Oh. *That* puppet show. Yeah, um, I remember it."

"It's the only puppet show you ever did."

"Yeah. That's true."

We looked at each other for a minute.

He cleared his throat a little. "Yeah, um, that's sort of maybe where my stage fright started."

"I didn't remember that you had any stage fright."

"Well, it didn't really start until after. Um. After you."

I finally realized what he meant. "Me? I made you have stage fright? Because of my question? Even though *it was the question-and-answer section*?"

"Yeah, um, there wasn't a question-and-answer section."

"Sure there was. It was right after the—"

"Nope."

"But—"

"Nope."

"Really?"

"Nope. You did ask a question, though. Right before my big finale. And it kind of threw me off my game."

"Wow. I am so sorry."

"It's okay. I mean, it was five years ago."

I stared at one of my dad's surgery drawings. I was suddenly afraid that this was going to lead back to Howe and me not talking. "Still. I'm really sorry."

"It's okay."

"That was so dumb of me. I don't even remember the question. Whatever it was that was so important, I have no idea."

He smiled a little. "That's funny. I don't remember it either. Just the feeling of being onstage and not knowing what to do next. It was the scariest thing that had ever happened to me. And every time I go onstage in front of people, I'm a little afraid, I guess, that it's going to happen again, you know. That something won't go according to plan."

"I definitely get that," I said.

We stood for a moment in silence and then he shifted, knocking down another picture behind him. This one he didn't catch in time, and it hit the floor, cracking the frame.

"Sorry," he said as he tried to fit the two cracked pieces back together.

I looked at the drawing in his hands. It was a close-up of something being surgically removed. Funny how you could just pop out an appendix. But there was so much stuff in us that couldn't be removed. So much stuff you had to live with, like stage fright and heartbreak. I was trying to get Em back, but even if she changed her mind, even if she decided I wasn't boring after all, I was going to have to live with the fact that she dumped me in the first place. I couldn't remove the things she'd said. Like Howe couldn't just remove his stage fright. Even more than our hearts and kidneys, we are made of imaginary things, I thought dizzily.

"But..." I said. "But I'm thinking—look how many brave things, totally off-plan things you've already done tonight. *You've been hanging out with the undead for hours.* Maybe this concert is worth trying. And you've already sung in front of my Grandma Van. Can it get much scarier than that?"

He hung the drawing back on the wall. It was still cracked, but if you didn't look hard, you couldn't tell. Howe bit his lip for a minute. "Most of the ... mature people are probably semideaf or semiblind anyway, right?"

"Probably," I said. "I mean, definitely. And I promise I won't ask you any questions."

He shook his head, but it was a yes.

Then, feeling a little bit like actual friends, we went back down the hallway and stepped into the lab. Where we stopped, mouths hanging open. Grandma Van was standing on top of one of the tables, reaching up to the ceiling, where she was taping some of the blue streamers over the harsh white lights.

Just to be clear. SHE WAS STANDING. ON HER TOES. ON A TABLE.

Over to the side, her scooter sat empty, plugged into the wall.

THE MORTIFICATION OF FOVEA MUNSON

"A little to the left," Lake was saying.

"AAAAAAAARRRRRHHHHHHHH," I said.

She turned a bit and spotted us.

"Well, come on! It's time to decorate!"

22.

HIPPOCRATES DID NOT GET OUTRAGEOUSLY FOOLED

Howe, Grandma Van, and I decorated, following Lake's instructions. The absolutely infuriating fact that I'd been tricked by my very own grandmother was making it hard to focus. "You. Can. Walk. And you just let Howe push you all the way back here?"

"I didn't mind," he said quickly.

"That's not the point!" I said.

Grandma Van grabbed a roll of blue streamers. "I guess I don't need the chair as much as I thought I did."

"And that's just it? What are you going to tell my mom, who thinks you have to use that thing?"

"Don't you think she'll be happy about it?"

She was right, and that made me even madder.

"Why use the chair in the first place?" asked Howe.

"That cushion fits my behind," she said. "It's like taking my own armchair with me wherever I go. And, frankly, I'd been pretty sure I was on the verge of checking out, so it seemed appropriate."

"And, what—*poof!*—you've changed your mind?" I asked. "You can't just do that."

"It's been a big night," she said with a shrug.

I didn't want to talk about it anymore. "Give me back those scissors."

While Howe and I had been in the hall, Grandma Van had searched the lab and made a pile of anything that might be helpful, which included surgical tape, big sheets of gauze, a lot of suture, and a stack of paper. Under Lake's direction, she and Howe were taping the streamers up, adding a little gauze here and there. Slowly, the lab was getting dimmer, bluer. There was latex in the surgical tape, so in the interest of me not having a major allergic reaction, Lake had me on paper duty, cutting stars out of paper and threading through them with the longest pieces of suture we could find. The needles on the suture were really sharp and curved, and though they went through the paper easily, I had to be careful not to keep stabbing myself in the finger.

Grandma Van made an announcement to the line outside that the party would open for business in fifteen minutes, so we were all going as fast as possible. As soon as somebody finished a job, Lake was right there with a new one. "Those shelves, there, by you, Howe—no, to your left—empty them out. Fovea, hang those stands of stars from the ceiling. You can use the emergency sprinklers and those surgical-looking things. Van, you roll the other tables over to the side and throw some of the big sheets of gauze on them. Howe, take the rest of the gauze and drape it from those shelves you just cleared. Fovea, is there a switch for those adjustable lights?"

I tried every light switch in the room until I found the one he wanted—it turned on a bunch of tiny lights attached to the ceiling by adjustable rods. Special surgical lights. Lake gave me instructions for positioning them, at one point sighing and saying, "It would be so much easier if I got to use my own hands. I think they might be in Tupelo, though."

We were like a machine. A total decorating machine.

"That's it, then," said Grandma Van when the supplies were used up. "Are we ready?" She looked around.

"Places!" said Lake. "Places, everyone! Andy, Mac, and I need to get up onto those shelves. Fovea, would you do the honors?"

After situating the guys, I walked down the Hall of Innards and pushed through the blue door into the lobby, switching on the light. On the other side of the glass, Em was distracting the crowd with a game of charades. When I opened the door, the game fizzled and Julia yelled, "We're not getting any younger out here!"

"Obviously!" yelled a voice from the back.

"Took you long enough," Em said under her breath. "They're all maniacs."

"Thanks," I said. "Ready to get them inside?"

She nodded.

"We are opening our doors for business," I announced.

"What?" Julia asked, pointing toward her hearing aid. "There's no place in the activities business for the weak-voiced."

I took a breath and spoke as loud as possible. "We're opening the doors! We will let you in ten at a time! The band has a strict hands-off policy! Anyone caught touching the band will be kicked out! Got it?"

There was a murmur from the crowd. I had no idea whether they understood me. I turned to Julia, hoping she'd calm down. "All right, you come in and wait right in front of that door over there. Don't let anybody go past you." She agreed, eyebrows raised skeptically. I let in the first group and shut the door behind me.

"This way," I said to the first ten, plus Em, bringing them down the Hall of Innards. They seemed to appreciate the artwork.

"Ooooh, I had that appendix surgery when I was a girl."

"Is that a spleen? Looks exactly like what my Ricky had taken out of him."

"I declare, I've never seen such a lovely small intestines."

I stopped them in front of the lab door. "What were the rules again?" I asked. They looked confused, and so I gave them a hint. "No touching..."

"No touching the band," they all said in unison.

"Okay," I said, starting to open the door.

"Halt!" cried Julia. "I'm wearing thongs!"

I froze, horrified. I tried to push the image of her underpants out of my head. "I don't need to..."

"Ladies! Who else is wearing thongs?" Of the ten, eight were women. Nine people raised their hands. "Oh, you, too, Ronald?" All the way toward the back of the group, Em had the same terrified look on her face that I felt on mine. Julia turned to me, the grapes on her hat bouncing. "So? What are we going to do about this?"

"Pretend it never happened, I think...."

"You won't throw us out?"

"Why would I throw you out?"

Julia pointed impatiently at the door. At a sign, actually, the one that read, NO OPEN-TOED SHOES. Then she lifted her sequined skirt, stuck out a foot, and wiggled five wrinkled toes at me.

"Have you been talking about your *shoes*?"

"Of course I have!" Behind her, all eight women and one of the men stuck out a foot and wiggled five wrinkled toes each at me. They were all wearing fancy flip-flops.

I breathed a giant sigh of relief. "For tonight only, no dress code."

The cry went up. "No dress code!" Then, while they hooted and hollered, I opened the door and let them file in.

The last one in was Em. As she passed me and stepped into the starry lagoonlike lab, I heard her say, just under her breath, "Wow."

Yeah, I thought happily.

Then, slowly but surely, I ushered in the rest of the line. With each group, I stopped at the entrance to the lab and had them recite the number one rule, No Touching the Band. There were a few more concerns about thongs, but now that I knew what we were talking about, I could handle it.

When they were all inside, packed shoulder to shoulder, I stepped in myself. We'd done a good job. The lab was completely transformed. All the cold metal surfaces were gone, and the room had become a gauzy underwater nightclub with paper stars overhead. The dim blue light made it feel cozy, even. Flowery old-lady perfumes drifted through the air, obliterating the antiseptic smell of cleaning solution. On the far wall, the sheets of gauze hung from the higher shelves, draped to look surprisingly fancy in the blue light. The lights over there were turned off altogether, so that everything above the gauze was in shadow, and the shadow was black-hole dark. Impenetrable.

The residents of the Swan Song seemed to be having fun so far; the sound of them talking was almost deafening, probably partly because so many of them *were* semideaf, and so there was quite a lot of yelling. Now that everybody was jammed inside, I looked across the room and found Grandma Van. Em stood next to her. I gave them a thumbs up.

The three of us started clapping, and the clapping spread, so that soon, every person who wasn't holding on to a walker was clapping, and the ones with walkers were cheering, and it was even louder than it had been before. I watched Grandma Van for the signal, at which point I turned to the wall behind me and flipped the light switch.

Like magic, the tiny bright surgical lights came on. Most of them were scattered like stars across the dark blue ceiling, but some of them were pointed above the gauze,

where the impenetrable dark had been. They became spot-lights, revealing four faces in the air, nothing but bright faces shining out of the darkness.

The band had arrived.

The crowd noise stopped instantaneously. An old lady near me hooted in approval.

Then McMullen sang one solitary, lower-than-low note.

Howe looked nervous, but managed a smile and sang his own note, a little bit higher than McMullen's. Then Andy, and then Lake, each with his own smile and his own note, each higher than the last.

If someone had pulled down the gauze, they would have seen Howe standing on the metal counter and then, next to him, three heads on shelves at the same height. But between the gauze and the lights, Lake had created a spectacular optical illusion.

He made us see something that wasn't there. It was positively holographic.

I glanced over and saw Em, transfixed. If it had been anatomically possible to explode from happiness, I might have been a little worried for myself right then.

The guys stopped singing and Lake beamed. "Ladies and Germs! We are the Four Heads, One Heart!" The crowd cheered, and he gave them a second before continuing. "And we would like to thank you for coming to our official album release party! Welcooooooome to the Cadaver Lounge!"

Then Andy counted to four and they began.

During the encore, I decided to take a break. The guys sounded great and everything was falling into place, but I was starting to feel the long night all the way to my bones. Even though Grandma Van had opened the alley door to pull in some air, the floral perfumes had stopped smelling so fresh and it was getting steamy in there. Plus, I was sweating under the thick foam of the kidney suit. I snuck out and walked down the Hall of Innards, the music fading a little behind me as I pushed through the blue door. The lobby was refreshingly empty, though I noticed that one of the chairs had somehow gotten turned over. Those mature people were out of control. And they sure did love their activities.

I set the chair on its feet and, as I did, noticed a slightly crumpled piece of paper under it. Probably fell out of one of their purses or something. I grabbed it and was halfway to throwing it out when a few sentences caught my eye:

... should liken my love to the flame of a candle! Probably a rose-scented candle. Or licorice. One of those, and then combine that heavy aroma with the heat of the flame like the flame of my passion, hot enough to singe the delicate hairs on your arm....

I dropped the letter right where I was standing. Gross. Unless some mature person had the exact same ooky sense of romance, it was undoubtedly one of Inko's love letters. The page must have fallen out of his giant bag when he showed me that fistful of notes he'd written. Yeech. I mean, I'd touched a lot of disgusting things in the last twenty-four hours, but that letter was in the top two.

I made myself pick it up again and toss it in the trash, and as I did, I felt a huge sense of relief. Not so much about the letter as Inko himself. I was almost rid of him. Soon he wouldn't be able to hurt my parents. And they wouldn't have to know anything about it.

I pushed the glass door out to the sidewalk, and the sound of the concert disappeared altogether, giving way to the relative quiet of the street. A few horns honked in the distance. I let the fresh air roll over me in waves. It was glorious out there. So glorious, in fact, that it took about five seconds for me to realize I wasn't alone.

Somebody was sitting on the sidewalk, leaning against the building.

No freaking way.

Whitney.

23.

HIPPOCRATES DID NOT EXPERIENCE A LOT OF ANXIETY ABOUT BECOMING A DOCTOR WHEN HE GREW UP

One time, maybe five years ago, on one of the rare occasions when my parents had a date night, Whitney babysat me. She came over in time for dinner, and as the two of us hovered over our grilled cheeses or our mac and cheeses or something with cheese that tasted great but smelled like plastic, we had the only real conversation the two of us have ever had.

"So, I hear you're going to be a doctor when you grow up?" she said.

I choked on some plasticky cheese.

"I don't want to be a doctor either," she said, twisting her eyebrow ring. "I keep taking those premed classes and failing them on purpose. And then I think I must be crazy and I sign up for another one, I mean, I set out to be a doctor, who wouldn't want to be a doctor, right? But something inside me just doesn't want to do it. I want to be famous. And you know, there just aren't that many famous doctors. Don't tell your folks, okay, because I still need that job, and I don't want them to know, and are you still choking?"

The conversation ended after that, because the cheese was for real stuck in my esophagus and Whitney had to drive me to the ER in her dope red convertible so the medical professionals could smack me on the back until the cheese came out.

I don't remember my parents going out again after that.

The dope red convertible was parked with the top down, right behind one of the nursing home buses. The two front wheels had jumped the curb, so the car was halfway on the sidewalk.

Whitney was home.

"You're back!" I shouted.

She looked at me and burst into tears.

What. Was. Happening.

I ran inside to grab a tissue off the desk, and when I got back outside, she was crying even harder. She took the tissue and blew her nose while I sat down beside her.

"Are you okay?"

She didn't seem to hear me. Instead, her hands worked to fold the tissue into smaller and smaller squares, the whole time staring at her car.

"Is—is your car okay?"

"As okay as it can be. A vehicle pretty as that runs on hope, that's what Dean used to say. Except I think it's run straight out of hope," she said, a fresh wave of tears coming. She could hardly make a complete sentence, she was crying so hard. "And you—you're—dressed—like a liver—"

"Um . . . a kidney," I said, and then bit my tongue. Correcting her was probably a bad idea. "But liver is a really good guess. I mean, whoever saw one kidney walking around by itself? And are you really back from Florida? For good?"

She took a couple of deeps breaths and halfway nodded, like maybe she wasn't sure.

"You can totally have your job back."

"Thanks," she said quietly. "Was everything okay while I was gone?"

I didn't want to lie. But the truth was kind of over-whelmingly disaster-filled. "There may have been a small situation with that cremator Inko Fredrickson, but it's totally under control now."

"What sort of situation?"

"Well . . . he came by and freaked out just a little because he couldn't talk to you, and there's a misplaced specimen, and he found out about it, and made some threats."

Her eyes widened. "What sort of threats?"

"Just like how he was going to get the lab shut down and get my parents thrown in jail. But now you're here and everything's fine again!"

"Er—I don't know about *fine*—"

"And the guys are going to tell me where the missing specimen is, so you can just let Inko down easy and mention that the specimen isn't lost after all."

"Yeah, about that . . ."

"I know I only had your job for two days, but, wow, every single thing about it is either disgusting or creepy or crazy. It's all yours."

She blew her nose again. "How bad is Inko freaking out?"

"On a scale of one to ten? I'd say maybe a trillion. He challenged your new boyfriend to a *DUEL*. But now *you* can talk to him when he calls, and maybe that will calm him down. Oh—your phone." I pulled my arm inside the kidney, grabbed it from my pocket, and handed it over. Whitney let the phone drop in her lap.

"It's not going to matter."

"What do you mean?" I tried to sound encouraging. "Just tell him, I don't know. It's not him, it's you. And that we have recovered the missing specimen. And then he goes back to cremating people. And their pets."

She shook her head, looking kind of dazed. I wondered if she'd been in an accident. Hit her head when she jumped the curb or something.

"I miss Dean," she said. "He'd know what to do about all this."

"Did he stay in Miami?"

"No...not..." She hiccuped. "Miami. Not exactly. Fovea, do you know, Dean was my soul mate. I didn't believe in it before, but I do now."

"Huh." I was lost.

"We were going to be famous," she said. "On that show *Make My Voice*. They tape in Miami. We were going to sing and be famous. We could win the jackpot and start a new life. Leave everything behind."

"But you didn't win the jackpot?" It was a rhetorical question. She didn't look like a person who had won a jackpot.

"We didn't even make it there. Dean. Um, Dean—" The tears came again, harder this time. "Dean went and died."

Holy crap.

"Right in the panhandle of Florida, we didn't even make it to the city of Miami. I buried him behind a gas station before I turned around and came back here. I couldn't have won that thing on my own."

"You *buried* him?"

She nodded, hiccuping.

"By *yourself*?"

She nodded.

I didn't even know what to say. "I'm sorry. Was it hard?"

She nodded, still hiccuping. "Emotionally. Very"— *hic*—"hard."

"Did you even have a shovel?"

She shook her head. "I just dug a little hole and put him in it. Took about five minutes."

"That seems awfully . . . efficient of you."

"It was a little hole."

Oh no.

"Just about this big." She held her hands up to her head.

No no.

There was a sour feeling in my stomach. "Please," I said. "Tell me that Dean was not a head."

"Dean was a brilliant man. He was a magnificent singer. He had this way of looking at you so that your insides became one of those caves that they find that nobody ever knew existed before, but suddenly, it's a real place, and it has like eleven new species and waterfalls and lakes and rainbows and trees that have grown for hundreds of years. He was hilarious and inspiring. I wrote him poetry. In the short time that we knew each other, he was my best friend."

"Whitney?"

"Yeah. He was a head."

24.

HIPPOCRATES
DID NOT LOSE HIS HEAD

"You stole a head and took him to Florida? AND THEN BURIED HIM BY THE SIDE OF THE ROAD?"

"That sounds so much worse than it is."

"No. It sounds exactly as bad as it is." I didn't remember standing, but I was suddenly on my feet.

"It was a perfect plan."

"It was not a perfect plan! It was a terrible plan! Half of your plan *died* it was so bad!"

She gasped.

My whole body was shaking now, and I felt like someone else was talking for me. I couldn't stop. "You wanted to change your life, that's fine. But when you pulled Dean into it, you messed everything up for my parents! He was their specimen before he was your boyfriend!"

"I know, I know—"

"You *don't* know! I spent all this time trying to save my parents, thinking that there was just a misplaced head in some cabinet somewhere. But there never *was* a way to save them!" I was having a hard time breathing. "Inko knows the specimen is gone, and I mean, Dean is *gone* gone, and my parents are getting sent to jail! There is no way out!"

"I didn't mean to mess everything up. I can talk to Inko!"

"And, what, date him again?"

"Um...I think there was sort of a misunderstanding about that. We didn't actually date. We met when he cremated my cat. And then we went out to coffee some, and he was comforting. Sort of. I remember him being comforting, but I was also really sad about my cat. I may have said some things I don't remember about love and stuff. But I was talking about my cat." She blinked her eyes hard, like they hurt. "I can do the duel thing."

I was so angry. At both of us. "You can't duel him. He's blackmailing you, which makes him a straight-up creep."

"But he's unpredictable, Fo. What about the lab?"

"I don't know," I said, resting my head in my hands. "I think it's just too late. Too late for everything. Dean's in a hole in Florida. The lab's getting shut down the moment

Inko rats. My parents will go to jail. I guess I'll have to live with my grandmother in the Swan Song."

The enormity of it hit me. "You should go home."

"I'm so sorry," she said.

"I know."

And I left her there, still sniffling, as I walked back into the building.

Whitney'd taken Dean. And my parents had been handling the situation. Trying to figure out who could have misplaced him, tracking down anybody who'd been in the lab. That's clearly what they'd been talking about yesterday when they went over to the hospitals. A missing head would have been a problem, but they'd have dealt with the fallout. I was the one who turned it into a catastrophe by letting unpredictable Inko Fredrickson eavesdrop on the phone call with my parents. Whitney had started the fire, but I was the one who poured gasoline all over it. Whatever happened now was my fault.

"Attention, please! Your attention, please!" I stood on the counter opposite the stage, and from there, kicked the light switch so the spotlights on the guys went off. They stopped singing awkwardly, and the crowd turned around to see where the noise was coming from.

"Attention! The concert is over! Please leave through the front exit! I repeat, the concert is over!"

"Why?" yelled the heckling old man from before.

I looked over their heads, straight across at Andy. "We are closed for business. Officially, permanently closed."

I left Howe and Em at the front door helping the last few old people as they trickled out. Howe was supposed to make sure Em didn't wander back now that the lab was being undecorated.

Then I walked back down the Hall of Innards. Grandma Van was in her chair again, pulling down the streamers strand by strand. Harsh white streaks of light broke through the hazy underwater.

"Fovea!" cried Lake. "That was only our second encore! We had at least one more in us! Maybe more!"

"Normally, I'd disagree with him on principle, but he's right," said McMullen.

"It was quite... abrupt," said Andy. "Is everything all right?"

I looked at them for a moment, too upset to speak. They were still in their places, and flushed with the excitement of performing. I'd done so much to make this happen for them. And the whole time they knew.

"Whitney came back," I said. "Alone."

"Alone?" Andy asked. The question hung in the air.

"Alone," I said again.

"But *completely* alone?" asked Lake.

I crossed my arms. "When were you going to tell me?

After I'd done everything you asked for? Or were you just going to lie?"

"Fovea..." Andy let the thought hang.

"No, tell me." I didn't even know I could be this angry. "What can you possibly say to make this better? Why would you do this to my parents? To me? You *knew*. My parents are going *to go to jail*."

"Dear girl—" Lake started to say.

"You know what?" I said, cutting him off. "Don't bother. Don't try to smooth it over. I get it now. You were just stalling until I got through your stupid favor. You were all out for yourselves. You aren't my friends, you never were, and I don't want to talk about it anymore. Grandma Van, do you mind?" I carefully handed her the oven mitts. And I walked out of the lab, down the Hall of Innards, wondering if I'd feel this bad if my heart was in Detroit.

25.

HIPPOCRATES
DID NOT THROW
IN THE TOWEL

I stepped into the cadaver lab lobby and saw Em and Howe locking up as the last of the Swan Song's residents shuffled down the sidewalk outside. A quick glance past them confirmed that Whitney's red convertible was gone. Howe sank into one of the waiting chairs and I sat on the desk. Em leaned against the locked door with a giant grin on her face.

"So, Eyeballs," she said. "Tonight was awesome."

Fifteen minutes ago, I would have exploded into a thousand molecules of hope. Now, after everything, Em and our squashed-up-thrown-out friendship was only the second most important thing in my life. I *missed* her, down to my guts, but it was still a lousy trade-off for losing my parents. On the other hand, I was going to need a friend more than ever.

And Em looked so happy. "Do you think she'll let me work there for the summer?"

"Wait," I said. "What are we talking about?"

"Nussbaum's. You know, even though it's a bar? Is that legal?" She saw the look on my face and stopped. "What did you think we were talking about?"

"I thought—you had fun tonight. I mean, I know you didn't want to be part of the club. I know I kidnapped you. Technically and, um, actually."

"Eyeballs," she said.

"I know! You were right. But—I thought you were having fun. You know. With me."

There was a way too long pause.

She checked her watch.

Oh.

After our crazy night, nothing had changed for her.

Over in the corner, Howe yawned. "Why do you keep calling her Eyeballs?"

"That's what her name means, nerd."

"Not technically." He stretched out his long legs. He wasn't scared of her. Huh.

Wait a minute. "What?" I asked.

"That's more of a loose translation." He turned to Em. "Who's the nerd now?"

"Still you," said Em.

"No, go back," I said. "What are you talking about? Of course it means eyeballs."

"Not in the Latin," he said.

"Nerd," whispered Em.

"*Guys, stop*," I said. My head was swimming. I was too tired for all this. "Em? This didn't change anything? Between us?"

She shrugged. "We just don't have that much in common anymore."

I took a deep breath. "If you didn't want to hang out with me, why did you even come tonight?"

"I *told* you. I told you up front. I wanted to see the lab. Too bad I didn't get to see any body parts. But it was worth it to meet Nussbaum."

"So it wasn't about me at all?"

"Well, no."

And she left. I locked the door after her, too embarrassed to look Howe in the face. I knew what I'd see there anyway.

Back in the lab, Grandma Van had done a good job of throwing things away and putting the guys back in their places on the main operating table where I'd first met them. Where I should have left them.

"Come on," I said to Grandma Van. "We're leaving." I stood by the door and waited for her. Then I turned out the lights and shut the heavy door.

Howe stood to meet us in the lobby. "Em's gone again?" Grandma Van asked, looking around.

I nodded.

"And you're angry at the guys?"

I nodded again. "They lied to me." My voice felt thick. "That's mostly it. They lied. They said they'd tell me where the missing head was. And the whole time, they knew. They knew he was never coming back."

"You know where he is?" Howe asked.

"Florida. Permanently."

"Oh."

"Oh."

We all three stared at Herophilus for a few minutes.

"So there's a missing head?" Grandma Van whispered.

"Not now," whispered Howe. He nudged me a little. "I'm sorry."

"Me, too."

4:30 a.m.

I sent them off: Howe to the train, Grandma Van riding her recharged scooter to the Swan Song. Instead of leaving like I said I would, I turned off the lights in the lobby and sat behind the desk, soaking up the bluish glow from the fish tank.

I needed to be alone for this. I couldn't ask Howe, but I needed to know what that Latin translation was. At the rate I was going, I was sure it meant family traitor. Or monster. That I was born an Igor after all.

I typed FOVEA LATIN into the search bar and opened the first link.

Howe was right. The first definition was not, in fact, eyeballs. It was worse than I thought.

It meant PITFALL.

What.

They'd actually named me *Pitfall*. On purpose. This wasn't an accident. Accidents like that happened to other people's parents, not mine. Wordplay was their thing. Along with dead bodies, I mean. They meant what they said.

And when I was born, they'd actually looked at their brand-new wrinkly baby and said, "Hmm. She's our little Pitfall." They'd known what they were doing, and they'd been right on the money. The truth hit me like a heavy sack of Igor's knuckles.

I *was* their pitfall.

I was going to ruin them.

If it hadn't been for me, Inko would never have heard my mom on the phone. I was the reason they were in all this trouble. This was inevitable from the moment I was born. I wasn't just fighting against time and lovesick Inko Fredrickson and a favor-happy barbershop quartet of heads. I was fighting destiny.

I stared at the word "pitfall" on the screen in front of me, until finally I couldn't anymore. I turned off the computer and dragged my sad, disgraced kidney-self home to the people I loved and had ruined. As I walked, I realized I didn't care about lurking danger anymore. Herophilus swished easily in my hand, treading water in the plastic bag I'd put him in, since he was about to be homeless. I decided it was best, even if he had to live in a soup bowl for a little while. But it wasn't the costume or the fish that made me feel safe. I felt safe because of how pointless I'd become.

An early-morning rat ran across the sidewalk in front of me, pausing for a moment to give me a long, meaningful stare. *Pitfall*, it said. *Pitfall, pitfall, pitfall.*

26.

HIPPOCRATES
DID NOT PLAY HOOKY

"I'm not getting up," I said. "I don't feel good."

"Where?" my mom asked.

"Everywhere."

She patted my foot and left my bedroom. When she came back a little bit later, I pulled the covers over my head. I could smell her shampoo, even under the sheets. She told me they'd agreed I could have a sick day if I really felt sick, and did I really, truly feel sick?

Yes, I said.

It was a procedure day, she said, so they'd be operating all morning. They knew it hadn't been fun so far, but the lab would grow on me. Feel better. More foot patting.

And then they were gone.

I fell asleep thinking, This is it, this is the end of everything.

I woke up feeling even worse. Like I was made of sludge. But after an hour of watching the spiders fight the wind outside my window, I couldn't take it anymore. I needed to know what was going on.

I got out of bed and pulled on some jeans and a soft old T-shirt.

Daytime looked weird on the city now, too bright and peppy. Even the sidewalk was too shiny. It made my eyes itch. In the ten minutes it took to get to the lab, I started thinking maybe I was allergic to day. So I didn't notice that the door was locked until I pulled on it.

I pulled harder, in case it was stuck or something, but no. Locked. Absolutely locked. That was it. First sign of the apocalypse or whatever.

My parents were probably already in jail.

Wondering, no doubt, how Inko Fredrickson found out about the missing head, unless he'd told them, in which case they were probably thinking horrible, dark things about their daughter, Pitfall.

They'd be sitting behind bars, shaking their heads. "Should've named her Nobel Prize or Lotto Winner or New Car, or even Extra Piece of Cake."

"Nah," the other one would say. "No escaping destiny."

There was a sticker on the glass of the door, announcing 20 percent off reading glasses. Old-person graffiti left over from the crowd last night. I scratched at it with my thumb. If my parents *were* in jail, the lab was mine, I figured, at least until I had to sell the whole thing to pay their legal fees. Or until Inko Fredrickson cremated it. I yanked on the door a few times, knowing it wouldn't open, but I wanted to get in badly now. Somehow, being inside would mean there was something I could do.

I had a sudden thought—the back door. We hadn't really made it a patio like Lake wanted, but some of the old men and a few women went out there to smoke their pipes and cigars. I'd been so angry at the end of the night, I'd forgotten to lock it back up.

And now I wasn't quite angry. I didn't know what to call what I was.

I walked around the block to the alley, knowing that this route meant I was going to have to see the guys again, and debating whether I would talk to them. Probably so. I'd ask if the police had been there. Ask if my parents were surprised or just saw it coming. Except the last thing I wanted to do was make the guys think I forgave them, because I didn't. Maybe I'd wait and see how bad they felt about it. I tried the door, and it swung open easily. Of course. I mean, *of course* I left it unlocked. The lab I was trying to protect. Maybe subconsciously I knew it was pointless.

I stepped in, noticing that something felt different. No streamers, of course. No gauze curtains. No stars. But it wasn't that.

I took another step.

And realized what my parents had been doing that morning.

Of course.

It wasn't like this was just where heads hung out.

They were there for a reason.

27.

HIPPOCRATES DID NOT FEEL HIS HEART TOTALLY UP AND BREAK

Andy opened his eye. Just the one.

The other eye was covered by a strip of gauze that draped casually across his face, like he was a tree and someone had TP'd him. But he wasn't a tree and it wasn't toilet paper. The gauze came from *inside his head*, which had been cut open. A flap of skin covered the opening, but incompletely, almost carelessly.

It was horrible.

"Fovea!" Andy said. "Thank goodness! Listen. We're all very sorry about last night."

"I..." There wasn't enough oxygen. I tried to catch my breath, but I couldn't seem to do it. "I...I can see your brain."

"Yes, but listen: we didn't mean to upset you."

"Your *brain*."

"Yes, yes, we knew this was coming, but you can't make a good recording if you're worried about your brain dribbling all over the place. Or other...problems. Since we knew Dean's voice was going to be on that TV show, we didn't think it was going to make much of a difference when we told you."

"Stop! Stop it!" It was impossible to look at him and hear him at the same time. "Does it seriously not hurt?"

"What?"

"THE GIANT HOLE IN YOUR HEAD."

"That?" He looked toward the flap. "No, no. It's a little chilly, I guess. But it's what we signed up for. No surprises here."

The other two guys started to stir. "Oh," Andy said quickly, "maybe a couple of surprises."

"Fovea!" Lake exclaimed. Someone had made an attempt at sewing him back up, so there were stitches criss-crossing his head, Frankenstein-style. "¡Qué bueno verte!"

"What?" I asked.

"He speaks Spanish now," McMullen said, sounding amused.

"¡Es verdad!" Lake added.

"Well, *I* don't speak Spanish," I told Lake. "Just English and one semester of French. So my French is mostly limited to stuff about pastries."

"Ayyy, dulces," he said with a big smile on his face. "Me hacen falta los dulces."

"No, he can *only* speak Spanish," McMullen explained. At least the old grouch seemed whole-ish. Completely sewn up, and by somebody who actually knew how to sew, it looked like.

"Are *you* all right?" I asked him.

He didn't answer, just looked off into the distance past me.

"McMullen?"

"Oh, me?"

"Yes."

"Well, I have a slight change in my eyesight."

"What kind of change?"

"I don't have any of it anymore."

"You're *blind*?"

"Yep."

"My parents will fix it. They'll fix it." My parents. I'd completely forgotten to ask about them. "Where *are* my parents? Were the police here?" I felt the panic rise up in me. How quickly could I get them back to the lab? Was it already too late? I'd go to the police station or the courthouse or whatever. I'd beg whoever was there to let my parents get out of jail so they could fix the damage to my talking head friends.

I suddenly understood why they'd lied to me. Why we had to get the recording done so quickly. They were out of time in the realest way.

"No—" I was lost.

"It's okay, Fovea," McMullen said gently. "You must've known this was going to happen."

"No," I said again. "No, I thought—I thought you were I don't know, like holograms. . . ."

"¡Ja! Soy yo, la princesa Leia."

"Holograms?" asked Andy.

"*Holograms*, they're made with these metal plates, that's how you bounce the lasers, but the thing is"—I was talking too fast, but I couldn't stop—"if you break the metal plate in half, both halves of the plate still show the whole image, and you can keep breaking it down, break it into a million million pieces, and the images, they'll all still be whole, and I thought, I thought, you'd be fine, that you'd stay in a refrigerator maybe, but you'd be *fine*. You'd still be *whole*."

Looking at them now, I felt myself break into pieces. I wasn't a hologram either.

"This is probably our last run, kiddo," Andy said.

"Ay, algo me pica."

"What if I put you back in the freezer? Refreeze you?" I was desperate.

"Está allí abajo de la oreja izquierda..."

"I don't want to get refrozen, Fovea," said McMullen. "Damned goose pimples. If there had been any ladies in there, I would've been flat-out embarrassed. Actually, there might have been ladies. It can be hard to tell."

Andy added, "This is all okay with us."

Not for me it wasn't.

Lake was wiggling his ears. I didn't know why, though, I didn't have any idea why he was wiggling his ears, and I wanted to know, and there was nothing I could do about his wiggling ears.

"It's all right," Andy said again, for the millionth time. "This is what happens."

"No. It is *not* what happens," I finally said. "NO. I spent all this time, years and years and *years* worrying about Grandma Van, and suddenly she's just *fine* and apparently she's *not* going toes up anytime soon, and I let down my guard, and then you, you, you don't even *have* any toes."

"Well," he said gently. "Somewhere. I have them, out there somewhere."

I had to do something. I was trying so hard to think of something I could do that I thought I might pull all my muscles. And then something broke, and in that space, I thought of it. The thing I could do. I ran to my desk out front, grabbed the drive Dirk had given us last night, and ran back. I messed with the sound system on the lab computer until I got it on, plugged in the drive, and pumped up the volume. It echoed, bouncing off the clean white walls and the shiny metal tables and the thin cold air. The room was so empty. Just me and three brokedown heads. And the sound of their barbershop quartet.

Nussbaum had done a good job. It had the feel of an actual concert, of something happening live. Not the kind of concert from the night before, with the old people hollering and singing along. But you could hear the mistakes sometimes and the laughing and the way they knew when they were nailing it. You could tell how much fun it was. The recording ended, voices fading away, laughing about some joke that McMullen had told.

I was surprised how soon it was over.

28.

HIPPOCRATES
DID NOT GET
SCARED OF DYING

"Just the two of us now?" McMullen asked.

I nodded, but then remembered he couldn't see me, and said yes, but fast, so that nothing else could come out of me.

"Hey. Hey, kiddo. This was never going to last." He smiled so big that his eyes, his sightless old eyes, wrinkled in the corners. "It's not about us surviving death, Fovea. Nobody survives death. We're the pins, and death, he's the ball, and there aren't any gutters. Just a fast roll and a slow roll. We can't stop the ball. The four of us, we each had something extra burning inside us that slowed it down, something we wanted so bad it kept us going a little longer than it should have."

"Like what," I struggled to say.

"Well, Lake, he wanted to be a star, wanted to be as big as his feelings. Andy wanted to drop into the music one more time. Dean had an incredible voice, better than all of us, but he didn't care about the singing. He wanted to be in a convertible with the sun on his face and a beautiful woman in the driver's seat. He wanted to drive off into the sunset."

"What about—" My breath caught again. This was all crap, it was all wrong. "What about Whitney? She wasn't just somebody in the car. She's a *person*. How is that supposed to make her feel?"

"I don't figure he *tried* to die on her. But when he was done, he was done, and she's just gotta forgive him for that. He already had one foot out of the door, you know. And one foot somewhere else entirely. San Diego, I think he said."

I wasn't glad that my parents had blinded McMullen with brain surgery, but I was glad he couldn't see me. I didn't like the way my face felt to me. "Are you scared?" I finally said. "I would be so scared."

"Nah," he said.

"How can you say that?" I wanted to shake him into being afraid. Just so he wouldn't go.

"I've played a lot of lanes in my life—"

"Stop bringing it back to bowling! This is serious!"

"Bowling is serious, girl. But listen, I mean it. I've been scared so much in my life: scared that I would land a gutter ball or lose a big game or jinx it somehow and let my buddies down. And I'm only just realizing what a damn waste that was. I shoulda just let fly, you know what I mean?"

I pushed my hands against my eyes, still glad he couldn't see me.

"I don't know what's going to happen exactly," he continued. "Maybe all of my personal electricity will fly out into the universe and go make stars. Maybe I'll wake up tomorrow as a baby snail. Maybe I'll be on a cloud with a percussive instrument of some sort. Maybe I'll just be like a breath somebody's letting go of. Hell if I know, kid. But I'll tell you what: it's nice to feel warm again."

I just wanted to keep him talking. If I could just keep him talking. "How do you even keep points in bowling?"

"Fovea, you don't care about bowling."

"Sure I do." I wasn't even convincing myself.

"Here's what I'm going to tell you from bowling: You don't have to know how to write down the score. You need to know how to go for it. Do you know what I'm saying?"

"Don't overthink it?"

"I'm saying you need to let that ball fly, girl. Life isn't going to wait around for you. You wait to roll your ball, and the game will assume you're not playing anymore, and those pins are going to reset around you, every time."

"But I can't, I can't bowl, I don't know how to bowl."

"Well, it's a good thing I'm not really talking about bowling, then."

"You aren't?"

"What's the thing you really want to ask me?"

My ribs felt so tight. Like my lungs weren't strong enough to make them move. "What about you?"

"What about me?"

"What burned in you so bad?"

He closed his blind eyes for a minute. "I wanted to make my son proud of me. All the time I spent at the lanes, and what did I leave him? A few ugly old trophies. I made him bowl with me, even though he didn't want to. I didn't listen to him until the 1997 Championship Game when he started throwing balls so hard they smashed right through the backboards."

"Bobby-Duran? Bobby-Duran was your son?"

"Yeah." He smiled. "Strongest guy I ever knew. I shoulda got to know him better. I don't know if he'll ever hear the album, but he always wanted me to put more good into the world. I wasn't very skillful at doing that; all I knew how to do was bowl. So this seemed like an important thing. Helping a few other guys with their dreams. Make some halfway decent music."

"I'll get it to him. The recording from last night. If you want."

He closed his eyes for a moment and then smiled. "Thank you, Fovea."

"I'll grab a pen, write his info down." I ducked out of the lab and ran to my mom's office, figuring it was closer than the lobby, but in the seconds I was gone, I'd missed him.

McMullen's game was over.

29.

HIPPOCRATES
DID NOT CRY

30.

HIPPOCRATES
DID NOT NEED PEOPLE

At some point, I called Howe. He got to the lab pretty fast, and since no one else was around to tell him, I did. And then we took the box of tissues and lay down on the floor of the lobby because it was the only thing we could think to do.

"I hope you don't take this the wrong way," he said, "but that ceiling is kind of gross."

"No, you're right," I said. "Actually, you know, the floor of a cadaver lab lobby is probably super gross."

"I don't care," he said.

"Yeah. Me neither."

31.

HIPPOCRATES DID
NOT COME UP
WITH SCHEMES

It came to me while I was lying there, thinking about bowling. Well, thinking about the *idea* of bowling, not about *going* bowling.

And specifically how hard it must be to be the first pin.

Getting smashed over and over again.

Everybody's always talking about the bowling ball, but what about the pin, you know?

The thing about the pin is, it always gets back up.

A pin would not lie down on the gross floor of a cadaver lab and get all swampy feeling sad. It would stand up again.

This situation was, as a great man might say, baloney. I was going to save my parents after all. The only problem was that I had no idea how to do it. Then all of a sudden I did.

"I've got it," I said, jumping to my feet so fast the lobby swam for a moment.

"Got what?" Howe said from the ground.

"The simplest solution. Whitney said she would talk to Inko. She can tell him it's not personal, that it's a conflict of interest. They each want different things from their dead bodies. Inko wants to burn them up, Whitney is in the use-them-whole-ish business. Then it's technical, purely technical. It's not emotional, and he won't freak out."

"If you say so," said Howe. "I don't know much about that stuff."

"I'll run it by Whitney," I said.

While Howe stayed on the floor, I poked around on the computer, eventually finding an old staff directory with Whitney's phone number on it.

When I got her, she immediately started apologizing.

"It doesn't matter anymore. Nothing matters except saving my parents." I told her I wasn't mad anymore, that we had one last chance. I tried to keep my voice steady as I told her that my parents were already MIA, probably being questioned by the police, that Inko's plan was probably in motion. And then I told her my counterplan.

"Will that work?" she asked.

"I honestly don't know, but we have nothing left to lose at this point. And we're out of time, so we should do it now. At the lab," I added. "To reinforce the professionalism angle."

"I'll do my best," she said. "He's hard to predict, you know?"

"Do you think it's a good plan?" I asked.

"I honestly don't know. But it's better than no plan at all," she said, not doing a very good job of sounding hopeful. On that note, we hung up.

"Howe!"

He was still lying on the floor.

"You have to get up."

"I don't want to."

I kicked one of his feet and he straggled to standing. I took him back to the conference room, and showed him the big closet with the other side of the fish tank. "You can watch from here if you want," I said. "I'm going to hide under the desk so I can hear better. It might get crowded if we were both down there."

He nodded, then noticed something through the tank. "Somebody's here."

A wave of nervousness hit me, and shoulder to shoulder we peered out from behind the castle. Somebody was definitely at the front door. Only there was so much of that dumb fake seaweed in that corner it was impossible to tell who it was.

I tried to talk myself down as I walked back to the lobby. Maybe Whitney was already here, I told myself, and that meant the plan was happening. It was happening and it was going to work exactly the way I wanted it to. I pushed open the blue door and jumped about eight feet in the air.

"What? Who is it?" Howe's voice sounded thick and far away. I could see him clearly over the top of the castle, gesturing emphatically toward the door.

Impossible. I held up a finger for him to wait and went to answer the door. She was wearing giant tortoiseshell sunglasses and a head scarf. She'd mashed her face up against the glass, and when she leaned back as I unlocked the door, there was lipstick smeared where she'd been. Julia Klinger. I made sure not to open the door too wide. "Can I help you? Did you leave something behind last night?"

The old lady pushed her way right past me, just as Grandma Van raced down the sidewalk in her scooter. She tried to take the door too fast and rammed into it once before zooming inside after Julia. I shut and locked the door quickly, turning around to face them both.

"What are you doing here?" I asked.

"It's unthinkable," Grandma Van declared.

"Butt out, Vanessa," said Julia Klinger. "This is my business."

"Fovea Hippocrates Munson, you tell her no," said Grandma Van.

But I didn't tell her anything, because at that moment, Whitney arrived, stopping to stare through the door at Grandma Van and Julia.

"See there!" said Julia Klinger, reapplying lipstick more or less onto her lips. "All kinds of people dropping in! It's a free-for-all around here."

Whitney let herself in and hovered by the door, keeping an eye on the street. I could tell by the look on her face that we had to hurry. "Grandma Van, this is not a great time."

"She said she was going to get her hair done, but I didn't believe her. Not as far as I could throw her." Grandma Van's voice dropped. "She wears a wig. Like it's not obvious."

"Ha!" said Julia Klinger. "Shows what you know. Sometimes *you have to get the wig done*."

"Well, that's not what happened today, is it? She drove over and thankfully she's very easy to follow, especially now that my chair's battery is fully recharged. So I followed her, and sure enough, she led me right here. She wants to steal my thunder."

Oh, my brain. "Your—"

"Thunder. From last night. That party is going down in the history of the Swan Song as the greatest activity ever."

"On that note," said Julia Klinger, turning to me and

pulling out a checkbook. "I'd like to book the space again. And the band."

It was like getting punched in the heart.

"The band has retired," I said.

"Why does everybody I know keep retiring?" she groused. "Wussies."

Grandma Van was gloating.

"Fovea!" Whitney gasped. "He's jogging down the steps from the train!"

We were out of time. I needed to get rid of Grandma Van and Julia, and pronto.

At that moment, Julia shrieked. "There's a boy in your fish tank!"

By the time Inko Fredrickson snaked through the door two minutes later, Grandma Van and Julia were crammed in the closet behind the fish tank. They'd agreed to a temporary truce, but only because they both wanted a view of the action, and there was no other place to see into the lobby. According to the two of them, there wasn't room for three people back there ("*Barely* enough for one," Grandma Van had said meaningfully), so Howe and I got ready to wedge ourselves in together under the desk. It was going to be an extremely tight fit. As we ducked under, Whitney stood by the door, ready to be apologetic but professional.

As we squeezed in together, I glanced at Howe, his face

about nine inches from mine and mashed up against one of his bony knees. We shared a slightly panicked almost-smile and then heard the door swing open.

"I'm here," we heard Inko say, catching his breath. "I'm here!"

The door swung shut and then it went quiet, except for the sound of him panting. This was torture. I needed to see. And I didn't have many options—just the two narrow strips where the front of the desk didn't quite meet the sides. I gestured to Howe with my eyes and then, without making any noise, we Rubik's-Cubed ourselves around until my head was pressed against the corner. I could see out into the rest of the lobby, but so far, they were both still too close to the door for me to see anything.

"Thanks for coming," Whitney said.

"Where is he? We'll have the duel right here, right now. I'm ready. Soon as I catch my breath. I've been ready for this my whole life!"

"There's not going to be a duel," said Whitney, and she took a few steps away from him, crossing through my line of vision. She looked calm. In control. Good.

"No duel?" Inko was starting to sound less winded. "You've changed your mind? You're coming back to me?"

"It's not like that."

"What's it like, then?" As he spoke, he stepped forward, so that I could see about half of him. "Can you possibly deny the raw appeal of all *this*?" He licked a finger and carefully smoothed down one eyebrow and then the other, and suddenly I regretted being able to see even half of him. I closed my eyes, trying to block out the revolting mental image of Inko trying to be steamy. Dear Lake, I thought. If you are a ghost now, please interfere in this. Please poltergeist the heck out of this lobby, stat. When I opened my eyes again, Inko had stepped out of range.

"Inko," Whitney said firmly. "We can't date."

"What?"

"It's a conflict of interest."

"Who is conflicted?"

"Me, working in a cadaver lab. You, a cremator. It's not meant to be."

"I can't think of any two people more meant to be! And who will help you study?"

"I'm sorry, Inko. But it's a problem, professionally speaking."

"Oh," he said, and was quiet for a moment.

"You get how it is."

"I do," he said.

"It's just not possible."

"Not while you work here," he said.

"Right."

"But if you didn't work here?"

"But I do."

"I thought you quit."

"That was a temporary thing."

"But if it was permanent?"

I didn't like where this was going. Whitney didn't seem to either, because she said, "We can talk about being friends, maybe. So if you could retract your complaint, that would be best for us all."

"Mm," he said, sounding distracted. "Do you mind if I make a quick call? Privately?"

"I guess not," said Whitney. "Come with me."

I was using all of my mental powers to try to communicate to her that this was a bad idea, but she led him through the blue door and they were gone. After a second, I untwisted and whispered to Howe, "Stay here."

He nodded and I crawled out from under the desk, stiff from being so crunched up. As I stood, I saw Grandma Van and Julia Klinger frozen, mouths open in surprise, on the other side of the tank. He was in there with them. Whitney had taken him into the conference room. I hoped that Grandma Van and Julia could stay quiet, but I wasn't sure it was humanly possible. Right then, Whitney ran back into the lobby.

"Why did you take him into the conference room?" I whispered. "What if he sees them? He'll know it's a setup!"

She looked worried. "I know. But I thought it might help if we knew what he was doing. I mean, making a call in the middle of this? Everything he does is fishy, but this more than usual."

The two of us stared at the two old ladies behind the curtain of seaweed. We watched as they had a quick, furious hand-signal conversation with each other and then Grandma Van held up nine fingers. Julia held up one finger on her left hand. Then one finger on her right.

911.

"He's reporting us to the police. He's really doing it," I whispered.

"He's still going to get the lab shut down," came Howe's voice from under the desk. "If you don't have a job, there won't be any conflict."

Whitney clapped her hands to her head.

There had to be something. I closed my eyes. An image of Inko filled my head. Funeral face. Soot-colored clothes. Love-letter bag.

"I'll be right back," I whispered. Whitney nodded as I ran toward the blue door. Inko was still on the phone, but I had how long? A minute? The door to the conference room was shut, and I made a wild dash past it, down the Hall of Innards, into the lab. I threw open the cabinet of gauze and grabbed enough to throw over McMullen and then safely pick him up. I ran back down the hall, holding on to him like a football, past the closed door, and into the lobby. Howe had crawled out from under the desk, too, and shook his head slowly.

Whitney's eyes went big. "Is that—?"

"Yeah," I whispered.

Through the fish tank, I saw Julia turn pale and start to slip sideways. Grandma Van slapped her, and then Julia slapped her back, and *come on*, I did not have time for that, this was a *situation*. "Hold his bag open," I whispered.

"What bag?" Whitney asked.

"What bag?" Howe echoed.

"What do you mean, what bag?" I looked around for it. "THE bag. Inko's bag. The bag with the love letters. I'm planting McMullen on him. The police will arrive and he'll be his own suspect in the head disappearance."

"Um, Fovea..." said Howe, glancing around.

"He didn't bring a bag with him," said Whitney.

We all stared at each other in horror and then heard a dull knocking. Grandma Van and Julia. They were gesturing frantically through the seaweed, hanging up a mime phone. Inko was walking back down the hall.

Seconds. I had seconds. And nowhere to put McMullen.

It wasn't just that either. Howe and I were trapped out in the open, there was no way we could make it back under the desk in time, and we definitely wouldn't fit with a whole extra head, so I grabbed him with my free hand, spun around, and pulled us both through the door to the sun and the heat outside. We lunged past the window, stopping as soon as we couldn't be seen from inside the lobby and slamming our backs against the brick wall.

My heart was racing.

And McMullen was starting to ooze through the gauze.

"What's the plan now?" Howe asked under his breath.

"I don't know," I said, frantically running through scenarios where everything worked out, except I kept smashing right into reality. There was no way around it. "The police are going to get here and they're going to see me with McMullen and I'm going to get arrested."

Howe said, "We'll see about that."

Before I could ask him what he meant, Inko Fredrickson burst out of the front entrance, followed immediately by Whitney. I dropped to the ground and scooted behind the nearest car to keep McMullen hidden. Howe stayed and leaned, casually.

"Of course I won't call them off," Inko was saying. "Trust me, sweetie, this is good for our future."

We all heard the first sound of the police siren, telling cars to get out of its way. They couldn't be more than a couple of blocks away.

"That's my cue," Inko said.

"Where are you going?" Whitney said.

"No need for me to be here when they arrive. As far as

they know, I'm just an anonymous do-gooder reporting a crime in progress!"

I peeked over the hood of the car. Whitney and Inko were so focused on each other that they didn't seem to notice Howe as he slipped back inside the lab. What was he *doing*? No way should he be in there when the police came—he'd get caught up in the whole thing, and I couldn't be responsible for getting him in trouble now, too. I didn't have time to get him out *and* figure out what to do with McMullen and Inko. I needed two plans now, and I still had exactly none.

Inko took Whitney's hand and kissed it. She rolled her eyes. "Inko. You stay here and tell the cops you were pranking them."

"No can do," he said, and started to cross the street toward the stairway to the train platform. "But you'll thank me later!"

"I'm serious!" Whitney said, sounding a little desperate. Inko didn't even slow down.

The police horns were getting closer.

With a loud whoop, Grandma Van burst out of the office door, driving her chair full speed, Julia hanging on to the back. Looked like the truce was back on.

They flew off the sidewalk, past a stunned Whitney, and across the street, closing in on Inko, at which point Grandma Van shouted, "Ready! Aim! Fire!"

Julia, still clinging to the back of the scooter with one

hand, reached out toward him with the other. There was a small sizzle and Inko shrieked.

The Taser.

He wobbled and went down. Grandma Van swung her chair around as I stood. When she caught sight of me, she yelled, "Now what?"

"I don't know!" I said, adjusting my grip on McMullen. We all watched as Inko groaned and rolled against a parking meter.

"He should be unconscious longer. Victoria must not have fully charged the dang thing." Grandma Van frowned and took the Taser from Julia.

"That's Victoria's?" asked Julia. "That woman drives me up a wall."

"Um, guys," I said as Inko started to pull himself up the parking meter.

"Victoria means well, but I swear," said Grandma Van. "Always talking about that trip to Argentina with her tango instructor—"

"If I have to hear one more thing about the paso doble—"

"It's like, we see what you're doing, Victoria—"

"Hey!" said Inko, pointing a finger at the two old ladies. "You!"

Apparently recovered from the partial Tasing, he charged at Grandma Van. She motored off in one direction while Julia, screeching as she went, hopped off the chair, and ran in the opposite direction, past me, to her car. There was a lot of yelling, including by me, as I tried to get Howe's attention. If the Taser wasn't working, we might need a new weapon and I'd just had a flash of inspiration: the crazy nail file that Whitney stashed in the front desk.

"Howe! Go inside! To the desk! Get the nail file!" There was all this loud honking coming from behind me and yelling coming from in front of me, and Howe was shaking his head, so I pointed inside and at Whitney and waved my fingernails in the air, until finally Howe gave me a thumbs up and disappeared into the building again, so I figured he got the message. The hearse—the source of all the honking— shuddered to life as Julia revved the engine and slowly backed the car all the way down the block. Grandma Van might have been right about her driving skills.

Across the street, Grandma Van was still demonstrating her own questionable driving skills, steering the chair in wide circles, just fast enough to outpace the ticked-off cremator. He was getting winded and not yelling so much, and Julia had stopped honking, so I could hear that the sirens were getting closer and closer.

Right then, there was a strange *poof.* I turned to see Howe standing in front of Whitney's dope red convertible, now with flames leaping from the seats.

"WHAT DID YOU DO THAT FOR?" I yelled.

"You told me to!" he yelled back, confused. He waved his fingers in the air. Oh God. Like flames.

"The nail file!" I yelled. "I MEANT THE NAIL FILE."

"I thought you were saying to set the car on fire!"

"My car!" shrieked Whitney.

Inko stopped, looked at Whitney and the car, forgetting, unfortunately for him, about Grandma Van, who was not distracted, and continued her portion of the circle, zooming behind Inko and Tasing him a second and then third time.

He went down again, yelling a few choice descriptive words about my grandmother.

The sirens got closer.

Grandma Van leapt out of the chair, ran over to the closest storm drain, and kicked the Taser down it.

I looked down at McMullen and then had one last thought. The one thing that might work. That would actually make McMullen most proud of me.

Either it was unbelievably dumb and would never work in a million years.

Or else it was perfect.

A police car turned the corner and pulled to a stop in front of the lab. Two cops got out, their attention on Whitney and her efforts to contain the fire.

I took a deep breath and gently put McMullen on the ground. I peeled back the pretty soggy gauze and grabbed a sturdy handful of curly gray hair. I lifted him again, set my sights on Inko Fredrickson, and then, as the fire raged, I decided it was time to let McMullen fly.

I channeled the strength of Bobby-Duran so my puny arm could get McMullen all the way across the street, and I guess I'd given him a twist, because he spun as he flew, his curly hair fanning out as he made a beautiful arc through the air. I almost thought I saw him wink at me, but it was probably just my imagination. He sailed and then landed smoothly, rolling along the street for another few yards straight toward Inko.

The cremator had pulled himself up once again, but was even shakier than before, and as McMullen rolled right into his wobbly legs, Inko tipped over one final time, screeching as he went down, which attracted the attention of the cops. They ran over, and as they discovered the head at his feet and quickly handcuffed him, the convertible fire started popping, and I took it all in, thinking about how I'd actually done it, and watch out, Bobby-Duran, because my heart was pumping pure adrenaline now. I threw my arms out and yelled at the top of my lungs, "I AM THE PITFALL!"

And then Julia's hearse came barreling from the opposite direction, down the street directly toward me, and before I could jump out of the way, that long black car slammed into me and I felt my body leave the ground. I must have landed. But I didn't feel anything.

I couldn't see anything either, other than blackness, everywhere.

I heard Howe yell my name.

I heard Grandma Van in the distance yelling, "You Armenian bat! You killed her!"

And then I didn't hear anything.

My life cycle ended.

I straight-up died.

32.

HIPPOCRATES
DID NOT DIE

(THIS MIGHT NOT BE CORRECT)

I MEAN I STRAIGHT-UP DIED.

DEAD died.

And as I had discovered just a couple of days ago, this was complicated.

For one thing, I was still thinking. And what I was thinking was this:

I am dead.

I'm dead.

That makes sense. I got hit by a car and I'm dead.

Dead, dead, dead.

This is dead.

Weird.

I had been so caught up, you know, in everybody else dying or wanting to die or theoretically dead but not actually dying, I never really *never really seriously* thought about being dead *myself* before. Somehow, all the space in my brain designated for thinking about deathy stuff was full.

And then suddenly, without warning, I was dead, and frankly, I'm glad I didn't think about it, because it was kind of anticlimactic. It's a good thing I didn't really have expectations.

I mean, no tunnel. No light. No vending machines. No afterlife guide.

"Hey, now," said a voice.

And even though I couldn't exactly turn and look, because I didn't exactly have a body or eyes, I sort of... turned and looked.

It was a frog.

Okay. There WAS an afterlife guide. And behind him was someone else.

Madonna.

No.

A hockey player.

No.

I tried to make my internal eyes focus.

It was...

Oh crud.

It was Hippocrates.

"She doesn't look like a jerk to me," the frog said.

"Shhh," said Hippocrates. "She's waking up."

What are you doing here? I thought. *Seems like the upside of being dead is that I wouldn't have to deal with you anymore.*

"Well," he said. "Technically we're just hanging out in the same place."

And who's that frog? I asked. *Is that my afterlife guide?*

"I figured for sure you'd recognize me," the frog said, sounding a little disappointed. "Oh, wait. How about now?" He looked down at his frog belly and then, concentrating, shook it a little, until suddenly his intestines fell out.

Oh, I thought. *I do remember you. Devon Kovach's frog.*

"Was that his name?" He carefully packed his intestines back in. "I think I might have some haunting to do after we're done here."

"Anyhoo," said Hippocrates. "What's on your mind?"

Well, I'm dead.

"Yes."

So.

"So."

Isn't one of you going to guide me or something?

"Eh. It's your call. What are you in the mood for? I could

get you fitted for one of these bad boys." He spun in his toga, letting it flare out at the bottom.

No thanks.

"Or," the frog offered, "you could join me and we could haunt that kid Devon. We could also grab something to eat—though it gets pretty messy with me, just to warn you."

"Or maybe you're done doing things?" Hippocrates said.

That was a good question. Was I done doing things?

Actually, I wasn't. I wasn't even close to done. I'd only just started doing things.

I'm not ready to be dead, I thought.

"Oh!" said the frog, surprised enough, apparently, that a little bit of intestine poked out. He didn't seem to notice. "You sure?"

I heard Em's voice, echoing in my head. "Boring."

Except I *wasn't* boring. Even if I screwed up everything, ever (which I kind of had for a while), I had something burning in me, too. My fire wasn't barbershop quarteting. It wasn't being a doctor. It wasn't being the greatest camper in the history of campers. It was just being Fovea Hippocrates Munson. Or Fovea Hippocrates Eyeballs Igor Phobia Pitfall Munson. That was what was burning. And I was going to rock it.

I'm definitely sure, I thought.

"Well, the pleasure was all mine," said the frog.

I pointed the submarine of myself toward the surface.

The frog waved. "If you get a chance, ask Devon Kovach how he's been sleeping!"

I pushed off.

And suddenly everything was so surprising and so bright and loud that before I could stop myself, I yelled, "Don't cut off my head! I still need it! I need it *attached*!"

"Do you hear that?" said a familiar voice.

"Duly noted," said another familiar voice.

My eyes adjusted to the light and I saw my parents leaning over me. They weren't in jail! And they didn't even look mad! My head was still swimming, and I was so glad to see them, it took me a second to realize how worried they were. I wiggled my feet and said, "Look! I'm fine. I'm back now. I've got a crazy headache. And I'm little bruised up. But good. I was dead, but I'm cool now."

They shared a glance, and my mom said, "We think you might have a concussion, honey, but you definitely weren't dead. They didn't even have to shock you." She nodded toward the EMTs standing by an ambulance, halfheartedly holding those electric paddles they use to start people's hearts. The EMTs looked disappointed.

"No, I'm pretty sure I was dead."

"Well, okay," said my dad, winking as he took my pulse.

"No, I mean it," I said.

"Okay," he said, winking again.

"Concussions are big deals, though, sweetie," my mom said, putting a hand on my forehead and inspecting my eyes. "Just in case you've got one, we'll need to watch you like a hawk for the next twenty-four hours."

Suddenly I could think of nothing I'd rather do than spend twenty-four hours hanging out with my parents.

"Can you follow my finger?" My mom held up a finger and moved it around while I followed it with my eyes. "Looks okay."

"Hmm..." my dad said. "She *looks* okay or she looks *okay*?"

"I'd say both!"

They were themselves again, and I smiled, even though it made my headache worse. Thank goodness they understood each other, because even after everything I'd been through the night before, plus saving the day and then dying for a few minutes, I still didn't understand them. I was glad they were mine, though.

My mom was suddenly distracted by something just past me. "Is that Whitney?"

"Holy cow. What happened to her car?" my dad said.

"It was on fire," I said.

"And by the way, why are you yelling in the middle of the street that you're the Pitfall?" asked my dad. I could see them both starting to take in everything that was going on around us. "We were about a block away and heard you yell and then saw you get hit and bounce off the car. What's going on around here?"

"I finally translated my name. And I get it and it's okay."

"What are you talking about, sweetie?"

"Pitfall, how Fovea means 'pitfall' in Latin. I don't want to—"

They burst out laughing.

"Okay," I said. "Maybe you misunderstood. I'm trying to tell you that it's all right that you named me Pitfall."

Now they were doubling over with hysterics. Classic.

I glanced around again, taking the moment to check out the progress on the rest of things. I must not have been dead for very long. Two firemen were carrying Inko Fredrickson on a stretcher and some others were spraying Whitney's car with white foam while the cops gathered around McMullen. Whitney didn't seem impressed with the job the firemen were doing, and was pouring one of those little purse-size bottles of water on the fire. Grandma Van was hollering at Julia, while Howe stood a few feet away and waved nervously.

I nodded.

My hysterical parents finally got ahold of themselves, wiping the tears out of their eyes. "No, no..." My father gasped for air.

"It doesn't mean 'pitfall,' it means 'depression,'" my

mother said, but then they both dissolved into laughter again.

Maybe I should have let them go to jail.

"No ..." My dad tried again. "I mean, it *can* be translated as 'pitfall,' but the anatomical definition, the one we were using, it's the depression in your eyes where the rods and cones are, where you see more clearly."

My mom picked it up, still catching her breath. "We thought of you, our baby, as the best parts of us, the part of us that could see the world more clearly than we ever could, the part that could make the world a better place."

My dad reached out and grabbed my mom's shoulder. "She thought we named her Pitfall!" And they both lost it, again.

My parents.

Classic.

And, I realized with another headache-inducing smile, maybe I understood them better than I thought. And maybe they understood me, too. I just hadn't trusted it before. I took a chance. "Also, I don't want to be a Future Doctor of America."

They both stopped laughing abruptly.

"You don't?" asked my dad.

"Future Nurse of America?" my mom tried.

I shook my head.

"Future Dentist of America?"

"Dad, no."

"Ooh—Future Physical Therapist of America?"

"Mom! I don't want to go to medical school. I don't know what I want to do, but I'm really sure it isn't that."

They looked thoughtful for a moment. Then my mom smiled and dragged me into a sitting-up hug. "Well, there's loads of ways to make the world a better place."

"Absolutely," said my dad, joining the now massively embarrassing but also pretty terrific three-part hug. "For now, you'll just be a Future of America."

"Where were you guys?" I asked as we broke out of the hug.

"Oh, it's a long story," said my mom with a worried sigh. "Short version: We've been trying to locate something that went missing. We were chasing down one last lead, a student from a few days ago, but she couldn't help us. And then we grabbed lunch on the way back."

"What are you going to do about the missing thing?"

"We . . . aren't sure yet," she said, rubbing her forehead.

"You know, it could be nothing," my dad said, scratching his neck.

Terrible liars.

I glanced over at the small police horde. My parents didn't know it yet, but everything was about to get a lot more complicated. Even so: complicated was way, way better than being accused of a cover-up and going to jail.

My mom followed my look. "By the way, what's Grandma Van doing here? Does she know that woman who hit you?"

"I think Grandma Van's making a friend," I said as we watched Julia and my grandma yelling at each other. They looked over at me, and then hugged each other dramatically.

My mom's jaw dropped.

"It's complicated," I said. "Sometimes there's a truce, sometimes there's not."

"Well, let's say hello!" said my dad as we started to walk over.

"You know," I said as we walked, "maybe I'm wrong, but Grandma Van might just be on the verge of a real breakthrough." I let them think it over as we walked to where she and Julia had been hugging. Now the two old ladies were checking out the firemen. "Mom, Dad," I said, "this is Julia Klinger."

"It's WHO?" asked my dad. My mom elbowed him and then they both started complimenting Julia on her scheduling abilities. While they were all chatting, Grandma Van wheeled around to me.

"Good-looking fire, huh?" she whispered.

"Perfect," I said. "How'd Howe do it?"

"He heard you tell him to start a fire. And then he found

a lighter and a whole bunch of tampons in the office. Very flammable stuff, tampons. He feels real bad about it."

"Good to know. And just to double check," I said, "you're not going to mention any of the details of this to my mom and dad?"

"No way," Grandma Van said. "Not if you don't."

"And you and Julia Klinger, huh?"

"I think we worked it out. Might try out a partnership, actually. We all did good work here, today. Although"—she leaned in and lowered her voice—"I do believe Victoria is going to be put out about the mysterious disappearance of her Taser."

I snorted. Grandma Van giggled. The next thing I knew, it was our turn with the hysterics. I realized as I wiped the tears out of my eyes that I'd never heard her laugh before. It was gravelly, but didn't remind me at all of the cement swans. Huh. The sound of my grandmother's laugh. You just learn new things all the freaking time. And right around then, Julia Klinger apparently mentioned something about a flying head, because my parents hurried across the street, waving delightedly at Whitney along the way, and joining the bunch of police officers circled around McMullen.

It took me a minute to find Howe. He was sitting on the curb near the fire truck.

"Pyro, Pyro, Pyro," I said, smiling as I sat next to him.

"Oh *man*." He dropped his head into his hands. "And it was such a cool car."

"Yeah—but the fire worked. Combating chaos with chaos, right? And don't worry about Whitney. I'm sure she's got insurance or something. Probably."

We sat for a minute and then he said, "What a weird day."

"Yeah."

"And I can't stop yawning. Car fires and flying heads and your grandmother doing something probably illegal—"

"Very illegal."

"Very illegal, and I can't stop yawning." He leaned back a little, kicking his feet out long in front of him. "You saved them. Your parents. You totally did it."

"Almost. There's one more thing to do." I glanced at Howe and we both smiled. "But it can wait."

We sat there for a minute, and then he said, "I'm not saying we should do *this* again, but do you maybe want to hang out next week?"

Around then I finally started to breathe again, for the first time in about four months.

Also, it was probably time to wash my hands.

33.

ON THE OTHER HAND, HIPPOCRATES WAS NEVER A TWELVE-YEAR-OLD GIRL

And a couple weeks later, at exactly three minutes until noon, I turned the corner, crossed under the train tracks, and stepped out into the sun. I'd gotten used to the street being quiet again, so I was surprised to see five beret-wearing delivery people standing outside the front door of the lab. Whitney was in the middle of them and the lead deliverer kept gesturing to the truck behind them.

"What's going on?" I asked as I walked over.

Whitney sounded exasperated. "They insist that we ordered six hundred legs. We would never order six hundred legs. It would take forever to get through that many legs."

We both turned and looked at the large truck. It was a really large truck. That was a lot of legs.

The lead deliveryman returned with some paperwork, which he presented to Whitney with a flourish. "See? Right there." I peered over her shoulder, and in fact, it did say six hundred legs.

"Well, I didn't order that," Whitney said. "If that date is correct, I was still on the road to Florida."

"Oops," I said.

They both looked at me.

"It's possible," I said, "that I accidentally ordered six hundred legs. At one dollar apiece."

"It's not our job to correct typos," said the beret. "We just deliver the number of legs you ask for. This page here is your invoice."

Whitney looked at the bill and went pale. "I can go ahead and confirm that there appears to have been a slight clerical error on our part. Can we please return five hundred and ninety-nine of the legs?"

"There's going to be a restocking fee," said the beret crisply.

Whitney agreed to it, and as we walked back into the

lobby, she said, "It's okay. You were new to the job. Also, your parents probably aren't going to fire you."

"Actually, I can't wait to tell them."

"Why are you smiling like that?" she asked.

"No reason," I said. I settled into the swivel chair and glanced at Herophilus, who seemed to be completely back at home in the castle. "Anything else I should know?"

"Inko's apology arrived."

"No way!"

She showed it to me. A formal, notarized statement of apology for any perceived wrongdoing, and a promise never to come to the lab again. There was also an *in*formal statement of apology specifically for Whitney, where Inko admitted that he got a little overexcited about things, and he would no longer stand in the way of whatever happiness she was after, even if it was with somebody else. He said his brush with death had made him more mature about such things. At first I thought he meant Grandma Van coming at him over and over again with the Taser, but then I realized that he meant McMullen. Even if you were a cremator, having a decapitated head roll into you was probably terrifying.

In the end, nothing had been proven, because nobody, including Inko, could explain how Inko had gotten the head out of the lab and across the street without being seen. He tried his best to pin everything on my parents, but the only evidence (him in the middle of the street with a spare head) pointed to him as a potentially compulsive body-part thief. When the police interviewed me and Howe and Whitney, we all mentioned that more than anything else in the world, Inko loved cremating.

Since there was no evidence anywhere of the other missing head, the police suspected that he'd cremated it, but they couldn't prove anything. The case didn't even go to trial. Inko got probation and paid a fine for having a massive biohazard out on the street like that. My parents paid a fine for not having better security and they immediately bought a very high tech alarm system. Everybody agreed that whatever had happened would never happen again. I sure hoped not.

Whitney nodded toward the back, where my parents were. "They're about to take off for the afternoon. They're giving a lecture on—"

"It's okay, I don't really need to know the details," I said. One surgery was about the same as any other surgery to me.

"And I'm off to Nussbaum's!" Whitney smiled. "She's calling today's lesson 'Micro- and Saxo-: When Phones Go Wrong.'"

After everything went down, Whitney discovered that it made her sad to sing without Dean. So she reevaluated her quest for fame and fortune, and apprenticed herself to Nussbaum to learn the mysteries of sound recording and mixing. It turned out that Nussbaum had been developing a series of lessons for the last ten years, she just hadn't really been that aggressive about getting students. And all of a sudden she had three.

Whitney was one.

Em Taylor was another one. Every now and then, Em would say hi to me through Whitney. I couldn't be totally sure if it was really her or just Whitney trying to be nice. I was happy for Em that she'd found something she liked so much. And I was sort of proud that I'd basically given it to her—but it didn't miraculously bring our friendship back from the dead. It turned out that was okay with me.

My grandmother was Nussbaum's third student, at least for a week and a half. When she eventually got tired of Dirk, she quit and decided to teach a class of her own at the Swan Song: All About the Philippines. On alternating days, Julia taught one called All About Armenia. They went to each other's class and the truce seemed to stick, mostly.

One time, I sat in on my grandmother's class, and she had me call her Lola Van, like I was a normal partly Filipino kid instead of a weird completely surgeon kid who was named after the Father of Modern Medicine.

Lola Van.

It was nice. I might try to make that stick, too.

Of course, I wasn't done with the Hippocrates stuff either.

Whitney's schedule at Nussbaum's was great because

it left her plenty of time to work the morning shift at the cadaver lab. She took the mornings.

I took the afternoons.

After clearing things up with my parents, I didn't mind it so much. First of all, being a Future of America was way better than being a Future *Doctor* of America. And I knew that I was so far beyond the Igor biz, I stopped worrying about that, too. Eighth grade was going to be great. I had a solid feeling about it. I'd handled blackmail and big-time threats and kidnapping and lovesickness and *heads*, for Pete's sake. Eighth grade was going to be a breeze.

It also meant that I was spending a little more time with Whitney, who was pretty cool when she wasn't running off with biohazards named Dean. She was sort of big-sisterly, which I'd never gotten a chance to experience before.

Anyway, on that day of the six hundred legs, Whitney and I checked in and then she left. A few minutes later, my parents came through.

"By the way," I said as they gave me drive-by forehead kisses. "I accidentally ordered too many legs."

"Oh yeah?" asked my dad.

"Whitney and I returned them," I said. "You know. For a small re-*stocking* fee."

They lost it. It took them ten minutes to leave, and even then, they were hanging off each other, laughing. "Miss you!" my mom said as they left.

"More than an appendix!" we all said together. I know. I know. But it was sort of our thing now. They liked that I knew what an appendix was. I liked having a thing.

I did what I normally did when they left. Called the Children's Refinement.

When Howe came on the line, I told him about the legs. I had to explain the joke to him, but then he laughed. He's pretty there for me when it comes to laughing, even when the jokes involve medical terms he doesn't get, or in this case, ladies' stockings. "Your jokes are entertaining *and* educational," he said one time. "What's not to like?"

When I was done with the leg thing, he had double good news to tell me. First, his mom had agreed to run a class at the center on how to build hologram lasers. Strict age limit. Howe said it was probably only going to be the two of us, and I knew Howe was just doing it to keep me company, but it was nice of him. I knew exactly what my first project was going to be.

A bowling ball. Simple. Perfect. A cosmic joke.

And second, Howe's mom agreed to give him some scheduled, structured unstructured time. I asked why they didn't just call it free time, but he said he wasn't going to rock that boat.

I got it.

I got him, too. And he got me. It was pretty spectacular to have a best friend again.

Plus, we had a mission. We'd been using Howe's CRUD skills to locate McMullen's son, and we were getting closer every day. Howe wanted to tell me about a new lead, but before he could, the delivery people reappeared at the front door. I told him I'd call him back right after I helped them.

Turns out, they'd been so distracted by the leg thing, they'd forgotten that there was one small box, too. I signed for it like usual, and the guy handed it over. The stickers on the front suggested immediate freezing, so I took it back to the lab. It was clean and shiny in there, no real traces of the magic. Just echoes.

And then there was something more than an echo. There was a tapping. It was quiet, coming from the direction of the walk-in freezer.

My heart beat a little faster, but I wasn't exactly scared. Not here. Not anymore.

I opened the first door and walked into the fridge section.

There was an arm on one of the shelves, and the hand at the end of it was doing the knocking. "What's up?" I said, not sure if arms could even hear. But the hand stopped and started gesturing. I walked back out, went into my parents' office, and got a pen and paper.

I slid the paper under the hand, then gave it the pen. As I watched, it wrote:

Always wanted to do a handstand.

"Okay," I said.

On the Eiffel Tower.

Whoa.

Heard you know people.

Oh boy. This one was going to be a doozy.

APPENDIX

(You didn't think I'd cut it out, did you?)

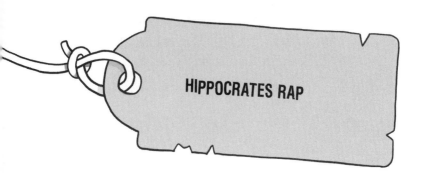

HIPPOCRATES RAP

Written and Performed by Franz Munson and Diana De Leon

My name is Hippocrates, I come from Kos
I am the inventor of the Hippocratic Oath
I'm known for my wisdom and my smarts and my
charm
But most of all I'm known for Do No Harm
(Most of all he's known for) DO NO HARM!

My birth date itself is a little hard to nail
Like lots of things back then, there's not much detail
The records are scarce if they're there at all
But likely as not, I wasn't very tall!
(Likely as not, he) WASN'T VERY TALL!

So I was small for my age, but I didn't let it stop me
I read and I wrote and studied sickness as a hobby
"Whoa," I said one day, "Hey, medicine is rad!"
And that's how I became an Asclepiad!
(That's how he became) AN ASCLEPIAD!

My dad and my grandpa were probably both docs
My family of physicians totally rocked
But the older I got and the more I learned,
The lessons I was taught made me concerned!
(Lessons he was taught) MADE HIM CONCERNED!

"Hold the phone," I said, "this can't be right,
Your theory of medicine is not airtight.
Getting sick isn't all about superstition
It's germs and genes and bad nutrition!"
(Germs and genes and) BAD NUTRITION!

"I have this idea," I said at the time,
"That the brain and the heart are connected to the
    spine,
That each organ of the body feeds into another
If we try using science, there's a lot to discover."
(If they'd try using science) THERE'S A LOT TO
    DISCOVER!

Now, I wasn't quite right, and you know that
    today,
But I did start folks thinking in a different way
And a few things I tried would pass a modern test
Like my method to drain a chest-wall abscess!
(His method to drain) A CHEST-WALL ABSCESS!

I'm quoted a lot, but to be quite frank,
It's hard to say what's true and what is crank
My advice to you, if you're not a porpoise
Is to read the collection called the Hippocratic Corpus!
(To read the collection called) THE HIPPOCRATIC
CORPUS!

[Note from Franz and Diana: We are still working on this,
so check back in with us, okay?]

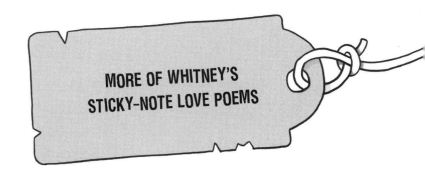

You're the sauce to my spaghetti,
I'm the footprint to your Yeti.

Your skin's a bit blue; my heart is well, reddish
I don't care at all that you're somewhat deadish.

Who's to say
What makes love work?
Is it promises? Is it romance?
Is it conversations in the moonlight?
It isn't feet, I can tell you that much.

Songbird in ice
You sing so nice
My heart goes kablammy
Let's go to Miami!

Two heads are better than one.
My heart is big enough for the both of us.
Thank goodness for that.

Head Zeppelin

Brain Drain and the Occipitals

Nasal Spray

Jaw Bones and the Soft Spots

Guns and Noses

A Head of the Pack

Whole Note and the Three Quarter Notes

Mandible Lector

The Headlines

Howe and the Get Aheads

Heading Toward Harmony

Lake and the Michiganders

ACKNOWLEDGMENTS

So many brains went into the making of this book! So many hearts! So many eyeballs. So. Many. Eyeballs. I'm everlastingly grateful for them all.

Thanks to the incredible community at VCFA, especially my brilliant advisors, Uma Krishnaswami, Coe Booth, Martine Leavitt, and Matt de la Peña. Thanks, also, to Amanda Jenkins and Tim Wynne-Jones, who read the first few words of the first ever draft for workshop.

Many thanks to all of Fovea's early readers (and listeners)—Rachel Wilson, Cordelia Jensen, Laurie Morrison Fabius, Katie Bayerl, Amy Rose Capetta, Eden Robins, Jarrett White, Emily Warren, the Gardeners, the Beverly Shores HTs, and the MC. Thanks to Varian Johnson for all the incredible writerly ballast.

Thanks to Ben Clark, Jake Garguilo, and Mike Wszalek for the holographic help. I'm grateful to Emjoy Gavino and Taylor Bibat for the long Lola talks. Thanks to Katie

Bayerl, Hector Bacarra, and Hector Toro for language chats. Thanks to my patient lab colleagues for answering questions like, what's the difference in thawing time for a ceph in a climate-controlled lab versus outside on a warm summer evening? Thanks especially to them for not getting me locked up after asking those questions.

Thanks to Rachel Hylton and Steve Bramucci, my left and right kidneys, respectively.

Thanks to the greatest imaginable accomplices, my killer editor, Rotem Moscovich, and my genius agent, Tina Dubois. I can't imagine Fovea without the two of them and their rad assistants, Heather Crowley and Berni Barta.

I am endlessly inspired by my parents, Karl and Malie. They are the coolest. Thanks are also due to my sibs, John and Paul. This book probably would have been way less gross without the valuable education of life with them.

My fantastic grandparents donated their bodies to science, and they're probably the reason I started this story in the first place.

And finally, thanks to Jorin, for heart-related biz.